"You Think I Didn't Notice How You've Changed?"

Jenny wasn't sure how to answer that. If he'd noticed, he'd done a darn good job of hiding it. "You didn't say anything," she pointed out.

"What, exactly, was it that you wanted me to say?" He leaned closer still, and a few beats of silence ticked past. "That your eyes look like emeralds without your glasses? That you have unbelievably sexy legs?"

Jenny couldn't move. She couldn't breathe.

His fingertips fluttered against her temple, touching her hair. "Or that your red lips look soft, smooth, delicious." His hand eased around to the back of her head, fingers splaying into her hairline, as he drew her forward, his mouth coming down on hers in slow motion.

What was happening? What was going—

And then he was kissing her.

He was *kissing* her.

* * *

To find out more about Desire's upcoming books and to chat with authors and editors, become a fan of Harlequin Desire on Facebook www.facebook.com/HarlequinDesire or follow us on Twitter www.twitter.com/desireeditors!

Dear Reader,

I was thrilled to be invited to participate in the Texas Cattleman's Club continuity series for Harlequin Desire. I've long been a fan of Harlequin's multi-book, multi-author series. I love cowboys, and I have some very dear friends in Texas. This project was great fun on so many levels, not the least of which was a visit to Texas while I was writing!

Mitch Hayward's professional football career has been interrupted by an injury. While he recovers, he's taken on the role of president of the Texas Cattleman's Club. There, he's reunited with office assistant Jenny Watson, who's had a crush on Mitch since high school. When Jenny undergoes a makeover, Mitch sits up and takes notice, and the sparks fly between them.

I sincerely hope you enjoy *An After-Hours Affair,* along with the rest of the TCC continuity series. I'd love to hear from you, so please feel free to drop me a line through my website at www.barbaradunlop.com.

Barbara Dunlop

BARBARA DUNLOP

AN AFTER-HOURS AFFAIR

Harlequin®

Desire

Special thanks and acknowledgment to Barbara Dunlop
for her contribution to the
Texas Cattleman's Club: The Showdown miniseries.

ISBN-13: 978-0-373-73121-3

AN AFTER-HOURS AFFAIR

Copyright © 2011 by Harlequin Books S.A.

Recycling programs
for this product may
not exist in your area.

www.Harlequin.com

Printed in U.S.A.

Books by Barbara Dunlop

Harlequin Desire

An After-Hours Affair #2108

Silhouette Desire

Thunderbolt over Texas #1704
Marriage Terms #1741
The Billionaire's Bidding #1793
The Billionaire Who Bought Christmas #1836
Beauty and the Billionaire #1853
Marriage, Manhattan Style #1897
Transformed Into the Frenchman's Mistress #1929
Seduction and the CEO #1996
In Bed with the Wrangler #2003
His Convenient Virgin Bride #2009
The CEO's Accidental Bride #2062
Billionaire Baby Dilemma #2073

*Montana Millionaires: The Ryders

BARBARA DUNLOP

writes romantic stories while curled up in a log cabin in Canada's far north, where bears outnumber people and it snows six months of the year. Fortunately she has a brawny husband and two teenage children to haul firewood and clear the driveway while she sips cocoa and muses about her upcoming chapters. Barbara loves to hear from readers. You can contact her through her website at www.barbaradunlop.com.

For Marcelle
in honor of our final writers conference

* * *

Don't miss a single book in this series!

Texas Cattleman's Club: The Showdown
They are rich and powerful, hot and wild.
For these Texans, it's showdown time!

One

Jenny Watson knew a bad idea when she heard one.

"It's not a date," she tartly informed her best friend, Emily Kiley, kicking off her shoes and curling one jean-clad leg beneath her on Emily's bed.

Emily called from the depths of her closet. "Just because he doesn't call it a date, doesn't mean you can't look your best."

"He's my boss. And it's a business function."

"It's a wedding."

"A Texas Cattleman's Club wedding," Jenny corrected. "And he was invited in his capacity as Interim President."

Emily emerged from the closet carrying something made of dark burgundy chiffon. "I was thinking this one." She draped the dress along her body, revealing a one-shoulder, sleeveless creation with a wide-fitted waist, and a two-layer, A-line skirt that dropped to midthigh.

"Ha, ha," Jenny mocked, leaning back against the oak headboard.

Emily knew full well that Jenny would never touch a style

that was so off-the-runway sophisticated, and she'd definitely never wear a color that bold.

"It'll look great with an updo." Emily swirled around to the corners of the room as if she was waltzing. "You can borrow my black rhinestone sandals. And I've got those fabulous teardrop earrings and the matching necklace. The diamonds are synthetic, but there's no way to tell."

"I'm not wearing that dress," Jenny insisted.

"Why not?"

"Do you need me to write you a list?"

"Come on," Emily cajoled. "Live a little, girl. You'll look gorgeous, and Mitch will absolutely sit up and take notice."

"I'll look foolish." Jenny wasn't showing up in front of her friends and neighbors in Royal, Texas, looking like some kind of Manhattan diva. "There's nothing wrong with my black dress."

It was her perennial favorite—a sleeveless, square-necked jersey knit that flowed to her knees. She combined it with a short, sheer black cover that fastened at her throat. It was the perfect combination of classic and chic.

"And how many times has Mitch Hayward seen you in that?"

"A couple," Jenny admitted, seeing no need to do the math.

Mitch didn't care what she wore. He wanted an uncomplicated woman on his arm, someone to help him work the event. Her boss liked to keep tabs on the members of the Texas Cattleman's Club. He prided himself on recalling details of everyone's lives, and Jenny knew she was a big help in that department.

"You've had a crush on him since you were twelve," Emily pointed out.

"'Crush' being the operative word," Jenny put in. And it had been over a long time ago. "The man left town when I was only sixteen."

Quarterback Mitch Hayward had gone to college in Dallas on a full football scholarship. He'd come back to work in Royal for the first two summers. But after that, his successful sports career had kept him on the road. Up until last year, when a shoulder injury had brought him back home.

"He's been back for twelve months," Emily pointed out.

"That long?" Jenny plucked at the bedspread, pretending she didn't remember the exact date, the exact hour, the exact minute Mitch Hayward had returned to Royal. "I guess time flies."

Emily plunked down on the bed beside her. "You are *such* a bad liar."

Jenny heaved a sigh, feeling the need to inject some reality into the situation. "I am not going to make a fool of myself by dressing up for Mitch."

"Then dress up for Rick Pruitt and Sadie Price." Emily referred to the bride and groom. Rick was a longtime member of the Texas Cattleman's Club and well respected throughout the region.

"Like they're going to care what I'm wearing," said Jenny.

Since Rick had rushed off to Houston in July to bring Sadie and their two-year-old twins back home to Royal, the ecstatic couple had eyes only for each other.

Emily reached out to grasp Jenny's forearm, her voice taking on a tone of urgency. "It's do or die, Jen."

Talk about melodramatic. "Do or die, what?"

"I've watched you pine away over him for a year now. Either make a play for Mitch, or start dating other guys."

"I'm not pining away."

But as Emily stated the bald truth, Jenny felt her chest tighten and her stomach contract with apprehension. All year long, she'd tried desperately to ignore her attraction to Mitch, telling herself it was a childhood crush that she was long since over.

"You're about to turn thirty," said Emily.

"So are you."

"That's right. And I have a plan."

"A plan for turning thirty?"

"A plan for my life," said Emily, her gaze taking on a dreamy quality and drifting to the window behind Jenny. "If I don't meet a man, *the* man..." Then she frowned, and her eyes narrowed. "Well, at least a man who might be the man, by my birthday next month, I'm going to have a baby anyway."

Jenny straightened in shock. She couldn't believe what she was hearing. "A single mom? Are you kidding me? Do you have any idea—"

"I want children."

"I know from experience how bad that can turn out."

"We're not talking about your childhood." Emily glanced at her watch and hopped up from the bed. "In fact, we're still talking about the wedding tonight. I can tell you, if I had a thing for a guy like Mitch, and if that guy was anywhere within a hundred miles of here, I'd damn well be doing something about it."

"You would not."

"I would." Emily nodded decisively. "Come on, Jen. What's the risk? He doesn't notice, no harm done. You simply showed up to some friends' wedding in a nice dress. But if he notices, it's a whole new ball game."

"If he doesn't notice," Jenny began, telling herself it was an academic argument, since she wasn't really considering the dress, "then it's game over."

Compassion rose in Emily's blue eyes. "If he doesn't notice you in this, it was game over anyway. Wouldn't you rather know?"

Jenny started to shake her head, but then she stopped. Did she truly want to spend the next year, or two, or three, longing for a man who wasn't remotely interested in her? Would she rather keep the fantasy alive, or would she rather face the truth, no matter how hurtful?

"If he's not into you, Jen, then you can move on. You have to move on."

Jenny catalogued her options, considering every angle as dispassionately as humanly possible. But, despite her efforts to be strictly analytical, her emotions crowded in. Her heart rate increased, heat prickling her skin, as she silently admitted Emily's advice had merit.

Perhaps it truly was now or never.

"Be a woman about it," said Emily, holding the dress forward, an expression of hopeful encouragement in her eyes.

Jenny steeled her nerves.

She took a bracing breath and rose from the bed, snatching the dress from Emily's grasp. "I can't believe I'm doing this."

"Shower first," cautioned Emily, taking back the dress. "And shave your legs. We have exactly four hours to completely make you over."

"I'm not—"

Emily gave her a gentle shove toward the bathroom. "Oh, yes, you *are*."

By the time Emily had styled Jenny's hair, applied her makeup, helped her into the dress and clipped on some jewelry, Jenny was a nervous wreck. Emily had refused to let her look in the mirror until the process was complete, and Jenny now stood in the middle of the bedroom balancing on dainty, high-heeled sandals. The fancy dress rustled against her thighs. Her face was tight with carefully applied makeup. And she had walked through a mist of Emily's most expensive perfume.

Finally, Emily stood back to survey her. "You ready?"

"I've been ready for three hours."

Emily's grin went from ear to ear. "You look amazing."

"I'm going to fall off the shoes."

"No, you won't."

"I hate wearing my contacts."

"Buck up. This is going to be worth it."

"The black dress would have been perfectly fine."

"The black dress wouldn't have changed your life."

Jenny frowned at her friend. Nobody's life was getting changed tonight. Mitch wasn't going to spy her from across the Texas Cattleman's Club hall, realize he'd never seen the real Jenny before and rush to pull her into his arms.

Never going to happen.

Which was depressing.

After tonight, she'd never be able to delude herself again.

"Here we go," said Emily, pulling her walk-in closet door closed to line up the full-length mirror.

Jenny looked into the mirror. Her eyes focused, and she blinked in astonishment.

The woman staring back didn't look anything like her.

"Something's wrong," she said to Emily.

"Huh?"

"That's not me."

Emily laughed. "*That* most certainly is you."

Jenny shifted experimentally. The sandals elongated her calves, tanned from swimming in the lake all summer. Her neck looked longer than usual, her arms more graceful, and the updo of her thick strawberry blond hair was complemented by Emily's glamorous earrings. The necklace winked at her, while her artificially lengthened lashes blinked heavily over her green eyes.

The neck of the dress made the most of her cleavage. And her bare shoulder felt decadently sexy. For some reason, her waist seemed narrower than usual. Maybe it was the full skirt, or the way the cut of the bodice accentuated her breasts.

Nervous sweat popped out on her brow. "I can't go out like this."

"What? Afraid you'll stop traffic?"

"Afraid I'll get propositioned."

"Good grief. You look like a movie star, not a hooker."

"I feel like a hooker."

"Yeah? Tell me, what does a hooker feel like?" Emily pulled a small jeweled purse out of her top drawer and snagged Jenny's bag from where she'd dropped it on the bay window's padded bench seat.

"This isn't funny." Panic began to swell in Jenny.

The makeover was all fine and good as a fantasy, but there

was no way she could leave Emily's house looking like this. The gossip would swirl around Royal for months to come.

How could she have let this happen?

How could she have been so foolish?

She swallowed. "We have to take it off."

"There's no time."

"There's—"

"If you don't leave now, the bride will beat you to the church." Emily stuffed the vital contents of Jenny's bag into the jeweled clutch.

"I'm serious, Em."

"So am I." Emily pressed the purse into Jenny's hand and held out her car keys. "You gotta go."

"But—"

"You want to be late?"

"Of course not." Jenny prided herself on her meticulous punctuality. And even if she didn't, she'd never insult such a respected TCC member by rushing in at the last minute for his wedding.

Emily gave her a gentle shove toward the door. "Have a great time, Cinderella."

Mitch Hayward was going to be late. Of all the days, of all the events, of all the stupid, stupid fiascos, it had to be this. At this rate, Rick and Sadie would be standing under the Leadership, Justice and Peace plaque at the Texas Cattleman's Club clubhouse with a preacher pronouncing them man and wife, by the time Mitch made it into the parking lot.

He zipped past the diner in his vintage red Corvette and geared down for the corner at River Road, his back tires breaking loose against the hot asphalt. But he stomped defiantly on the gas pedal, muscled the car to head straight and prayed that Officer Brendall wasn't out on traffic patrol at this particular moment.

The roof of the clubhouse came into view in the distance

amongst the oak trees, at the same time as he spotted a long white limousine on the road in front of him. It had to be Sadie and her bridesmaids. He geared down and put the pedal to the floor, pulling around the limousine, hoping against hope that Sadie would forgive him for the stunt.

He screeched to a halt in the clubhouse lot, parking illegally before springing from the car and running up the stairs.

His assistant, Jenny Watson, was waiting by the door to the foyer.

He was conscious of a flash of bold burgundy, before snagging her arm and towing her toward the club lounge entrance.

"What happened?" she rasped, trotting to keep up with him.

"A flock of flamingos," he growled, scanning the rows of folding chairs for vacancies.

"What?"

He spotted a pair at the opposite side of the flower-and-candle-bedecked room, and he beelined for them.

"Those plastic flamingos for the charity fundraiser," he whispered to her, ignoring the censorious stares sent his way by the Texas Cattleman's Club members assembled for the wedding. "The whole flock was planted on my front lawn."

He plunked Jenny into a chair and seated himself, just as the piano music changed, and all heads turned to watch the first bridesmaid start her way down the aisle.

The attendants were pretty in pale lilac dresses, but Sadie and Rick's two-year-old twin daughters all but stole the show. They were dressed identically in ivory lace dresses, accented with lilac ribbons and bows. They had flowers braided into their hair, and they dutifully dropped multicolored handfuls of rose petals from their baskets as they walked.

Then the pianist began the wedding march, and the guests rose as Sadie appeared in a stunning white gown, flowers woven into her hair, and a tremulous smile on her face as she approached Rick. Mitch was about as far from a romantic as a guy could get, but even he couldn't help feeling a warm glow for the couple who had been through so much, were so obviously in love and were about to create a family with their two young daughters.

As the preacher pronounced the couple man and wife, the guests spontaneously burst into applause. And by the time Rick kissed his bride, most of the women, and even some of the men, were wiping misty eyes while they smiled with pure joy. Camera flashes went off and Rick and Sadie each picked up one of their daughters to make their way back down the aisle.

"That was lovely," said Jenny, tucking her tissue back into her compact purse.

"You can't help but be happy for them," Mitch replied.

Then she pressed an elbow into his ribs. "Did the game go into overtime or something?"

"Sorry," he apologized, his mind going back to the debacle of getting out of his driveway.

Truth was, he had been further delayed when a football buddy, Jeffrey Porter, his teammate on the Texas Tigers, had called on the road from Chicago. Jeffrey's girlfriend of two years had caught him cheating and abruptly ended the relationship.

Mitch was intimately familiar with the temptation of beautiful women when a guy was on the road with the team. There was never a shortage of dates. It was one of the reasons Mitch had always avoided serious romantic relationships. If he couldn't trust himself to be faithful, he wasn't going to make any promises to anyone.

It was probably past time someone called Jeffrey on his behavior. Quite frankly, with the way his attention strayed, Mitch was surprised his buddy hadn't been caught long before this. Still, he'd felt duty bound to sympathize with the wide receiver.

"What happened?" Jenny asked as the front rows of guests began surging down the aisle, following the wedding party out into the foyer.

"It was mostly the flamingos." Mitch repeated the part of the story he'd decided to use as an excuse, while they waited their turn to exit the lounge. "Somebody obviously paid to have the flock planted on my lawn, and it was all I could do to navigate through the mess."

She looked up at him, skepticism clear as her brows lifted above her green eyes. "What? Did they gang up on you?"

He did a double take. There was something different about Jenny today. He tried to put his finger on it.

"I took one of them out," he grumbled. He'd been in a hurry after his phone call with Jeffrey, and one of the flamingos had scratched the front bumper of his 'Vette. He sure hoped he didn't have to repaint.

"Did you hurt it?" Jenny asked with a carefully schooled, straight face. It was obvious she found the mishap amusing.

"It'll live," he responded without missing a beat. "You know, I'd have given them an extra donation without the birds," he griped. A time-honored local form of extortion, the recipient of the flamingos was compelled to pay a donation to get the birds moved to another unwitting victim's yard. "A phone call would have worked just as well." He was a strong supporter of the local women's shelter that ran the flamingo fundraiser, and he'd have happily bumped up his annual contribution.

"The flamingos are more fun," said Jenny, turning as the people toward the middle aisle started to move. "I'll help you pick the new target. Maybe we can plant them on Cole's lawn next." Cole Maddison, Mitch's friend, neighbor and fellow TCC board member had deep pockets.

"Sure," Mitch answered absently, still trying to figure out what was different about her.

The glasses.

She wasn't wearing her glasses.

That was unusual for Jenny.

He wondered if she'd forgotten them, or if she'd decided the wedding was an occasion formal enough to warrant wearing her contacts. He knew she didn't like them.

She started to walk away, and his gaze caught on her short dress. That was also unusual. She normally wore knee-length skirts, or slacks, a crisp blouse and a blazer. Jenny was as buttoned-up and tailored as a woman could get. It suited her precise and meticulous personality. But today, puffy, bold burgundy fabric swirled around her thighs. One of her shoulders was bare, and she was wearing unusually flashy earnings.

What was up?

"Jenny?"

She turned.

Holy cow. From this angle the entire package nearly took his breath away. What had happened to his no-nonsense, efficient assistant?

"Yes?" she prompted.

"Nothing." He started to move with the rest of the crowd, embarrassed by the reaction he was having to her makeover. She was perfectly entitled to dress up for a wedding, and he had absolutely no business ogling her.

They made their way through the double doors, outside to the back of the clubhouse overlooking the expansive grounds. When Mitch stopped at the rail of the back veranda, Jenny kept going, making her way down the wide stairs toward the lawn and the gardens. He was a little surprised she hadn't stuck by his side like she usually did. Perhaps she needed to talk to some of the Cattleman's Club members or to some friends.

As Interim President, Mitch had been aware of the reception preparations for several weeks now. A few days ago, they'd erected a huge canopy tent in case of rain, but the Monday Labor Day evening was clear and warm. A band had set up on the gazebo, and a temporary dance floor had been built on the knoll overlooking the pond. Round, white-linen-covered tables dotted the lawn, and tall propane heaters were discreetly placed throughout the dining area to keep guests warm once the sun went down.

The wedding party had assembled in front of the clubhouse

gardens for photos. Even from this distance, Mitch could see the tension between maid of honor Abigail Langley and best man Brad Price. As the last remaining descendant of the TCC founder by marriage, Abigail was also the Club's sole female member.

It was no secret that Brad resented having a woman as a full member of the Cattleman's Club. He'd taken to using the term "cattle-people's club," and suggested they put up lacy curtains and buy a pink gavel for monthly meetings.

Most of the men brushed the jokes off as harmless, but Abigail had recently gotten wind of Brad's behavior and had been highly insulted. She even challenged him in his run for TCC president. Mitch got the feeling that she avoided Brad as much as possible. But today they'd been thrown intimately together as members of the wedding party.

He scanned the sharply dressed crowd, easily spotting Jenny where she stood beside the dining area talking to Cole Maddison. She laughed at something he said, and rested her hand briefly on his arm. For some reason, Mitch felt a surge of jealousy.

Ridiculous.

Just because he'd never known Jenny to date, didn't mean she shouldn't date. Hey, if she liked Cole and if Cole liked her...

Mitch found his feet taking him down the stairway and across the lawn toward them.

"Hey, Mitch," Cole greeted easily as he approached.

Mitch gave his friend a nod.

Jenny didn't glance his way.

"Nice ceremony," Mitch offered, wondering why he felt awkward.

"I'm not sure Brad's going to survive the night," Cole returned, canting his head in the direction of the tuxedo-clad Brad, who was on the receiving end of a glare from Abigail.

"She's a pistol," Mitch agreed.

"Excuse me a moment," Jenny put in, moving away.

Mitch's gaze reflexively followed her as she made her way toward the bride and groom.

"That's a shocker," said Cole.

"What?" Mitch pulled his attention away from Jenny's tanned legs and the sexy little sandals that accented her dainty feet. Her toenails were polished a bright plum, he'd noticed.

Cole's expression was incredulous. "I'm talking about Jenny. She looks like a million bucks."

"It's a nice dress," Mitch allowed, telling himself to get a grip. It was Jenny—sensible, efficient, professional Jenny.

"She's a stunning woman," said Cole. "I wonder why she dresses down all the time."

Mitch frowned. "I wouldn't call it dressing down. She looks completely professional at the office."

Cole drew back. "I didn't mean it as an insult. But you have to admit, it's a shocker."

What was shocking was that Mitch couldn't seem to tear his gaze from her.

"I may ask her to dance," Cole declared.

"With what intention?" Mitch demanded before he could stop himself.

"*Intention?* What are you, her chaperone?"

"Jenny's a nice girl. Just because the woman puts on a pretty dress, doesn't mean she's fair game." But even as he spoke, Mitch realized just how ridiculous his words sounded. Who Jenny danced with was absolutely none of his business. Neither was who she dated, or slept with for that matter. He was her boss, not her keeper.

Cole's eyes narrowed speculatively. "Have you got designs on her?"

"No, I do *not* have designs on her. We're colleagues. I see her every day at the office." Theirs was a professional relationship, nothing more.

"Not like that, you don't," Cole muttered.

"Quit obsessing about Jenny."

"Me?" Cole gave a hollow chuckle. "You're the one who can't keep his eyes off her."

Mitch realized he was watching her yet again, marveling at her grace and glamour. He dragged his attention back to Cole, meeting the man's smirk.

"Back off," Mitch growled.

Cole accepted a glass of champagne from a passing waiter, and Mitch did the same.

"Admit it," said Cole. "You think she's hot."

"I think she's efficient." And that was all that mattered in Mitch's world, no matter how tempting she looked tonight.

Two

Jenny's evening had been an abject failure.

Mitch hadn't been wowed by her new appearance. He'd barely seemed to notice her, and he didn't ask her to dance, not one single time. Through dinner, the toasts and speeches, the cake cutting and finally the dancing, she'd grown more and more depressed.

Now that the bouquet had been thrown and the newly married couple had officially left for their honeymoon, she was going straight home to take down her hair, take out her contacts, scrub off the makeup and send the dress back to Emily via the dry cleaners. She never wanted to look at it again.

Outside in the parking lot, she hunted through the small jeweled purse for her car keys.

To think she'd felt beautiful at the beginning of the evening. She'd let Emily's optimism rub off on her. Then, standing next to Mitch while the bride marched down the aisle, she had actually felt a little like Cinderella.

She retrieved her car keys as she made her way across the

asphalt, feet aching from the high heels and a blister burning on her left baby toe. Her car was parked under one of the many overhead parking lot lights, but as she approached it, she realized something was wrong. Her taillights seemed to be faintly glowing.

She quickly inserted the key and opened the driver's door to find her headlight switch on. She flicked it off, frowning, because it had been broad daylight when she arrived for the ceremony. She slipped into the driver's seat, pulling the door shut and inserting her key into the ignition.

"Come on," she muttered, holding her breath as she turned the key.

It clicked. The engine clunked. A brief grinding noise came from under the hood. And then silence.

Jenny cursed under her breath.

She tried the key one more time but was met with stubborn silence. She smacked her palms down on the steering wheel in frustration.

She did not feel like waiting for a taxi to take her home. And now she'd have to come back tomorrow and get her car. Though it was a workday tomorrow, she'd decided to call in sick for the first time in, well, ever. She was going to pull the covers up over her head and wallow in self-pity. She swore that a pint of gourmet ice cream and a sappy movie were as close as she was coming to activity tomorrow.

She scooped up her purse and reached for the door handle, when she noticed something on her dashboard. It was a folded piece of paper, and she was certain it hadn't been there when she parked the car.

Confused, Jenny reached out and unfolded it, leaning forward and squinting in the illumination from the parking lot's overhead light. *You'll thank me tomorrow,* it said. And it was signed *Emily.*

Jenny couldn't believe it. Her best friend had actually sabotaged her car? Had Emily lost her mind?

Someone rapped on the window, and Jenny nearly jumped out of her skin.

"You okay?" came Mitch's deep voice.

Jenny crumpled the paper into her palm.

He lifted the handle and pulled open her door.

"I'm fine," said Jenny, hoping he'd accept her answer and go away.

"Car trouble?" he asked.

She shook her head, still staring straight ahead. She just wanted to get home, away from Mitch and away from the humiliating memories of this night.

"I heard you cranking it over. Want me to take a look?"

"It's fine," she insisted.

He was silent for a moment. "Are you mad at me?"

"Of course not," she lied.

"Your car's broken down, Jenny."

She closed her eyes for a long moment. "I know. I'm tired. I was going to call a cab."

"Don't be ridiculous. Pop the hood."

She turned to look at him. "You're not exactly dressed for mechanical repairs."

He glanced down at his pristine white shirt and silk tie. "Good point." Then he held out his broad hand. "Come on. I'll take you home."

Jenny glanced around the parking lot, desperately searching for someone else who could serve as her knight in shining armor. The very last thing in the world she wanted right now was to spend more time in Mitch's company while he failed to notice the new, improved and sexy Jenny. But nobody else was around to save her.

"I'll just go back inside," she began.

"Will you *stop?*" He reached down and snagged her hand, drawing her gently but firmly from her vehicle.

She grabbed her purse and came steady on her feet just as he slammed the door shut behind her, obviously annoyed. Well, she was annoyed, too. Even if he hadn't been bowled over by her chic new look, he could have at least complimented *something*. The hair, the dress, the shoes. But he couldn't even throw her a crumb.

He kept hold of her hand. "This way."

She spotted his sleek, gleaming Corvette parked haphazardly next to the front garden. "That's not an authorized parking spot."

"I was late. I'll pay the fine tomorrow." He swung open the door. "Now, get in."

She huffed out a breath, and braced her hand against the back of the bucket seat, stepping one foot inside the car and nearly losing her balance on the high heels.

His arm snaked around her waist, and she felt her dress hike high on her thighs. Her bottom pressed against his leg as he braced her steady.

"I'm fine," she ground out.

"You're grumpy," he responded, a trace of humor in the voice that was close to her ear.

"Will you let go?" Her pulse was doing unnatural things under his touch. Her face flushed hot, and her knees suddenly felt unsteady. She determinedly pulled herself into the car.

He let her go, and she dropped onto the seat. She quickly straightened her skirt, covering as much of her thighs as possible. Then she glanced down to catch an expansive view of her cleavage. She adjusted the shoulder of the dress and tugged at the bodice.

Mitch had paused, watching her, the door still open. But she refused to glance up. He was probably laughing at her clumsiness.

After a long moment, he stepped back and firmly closed the door, moving around to the driver's side. There, he climbed inside without a word, started the engine and pulled the sports car smoothly out of the parking lot.

As their speed increased, the overhead lights flashed above them, alternating with the branches of stately oak trees lining the street. The silence stretched out between them. A mile farther down, they turned off River Road to take the shortcut along Rooster Lane. Given the potholes and sharp gravel on the little-used road, and Mitch's deep love of his Corvette, Jenny could only assume he was in a hurry to get rid of her.

Fine by her. She couldn't wait to get home.

Then, abruptly, he pulled off the road onto a grassy patch beneath the oak trees, rocked the car to a halt and set the emergency brake.

"What are you doing?" she asked in confusion, wondering if something was wrong with his car. Surely, Emily couldn't have sabotaged them both.

But he turned in his seat, draping his arm across the back of hers. "Spill, Jenny. What's wrong?"

His abrupt question took her by surprise. But she quickly regrouped. "I'm tired and I want to go home." That was definitely part of the truth.

"You've been acting weird all night," he pressed.

"I have not." She folded her hands primly on her lap.

"You didn't even dance with me."

The accusation in his voice made her own tone rise along with her blood pressure. She spoke past a clenched jaw. "You didn't even ask."

"I had to ask?" he retorted.

"It's kind of traditional."

"Like you needed extra partners," he scoffed.

She turned to look at him. "What's that supposed to mean?"

"It means—" he gestured with one hand "—the way you're dressed tonight, there was a line around the block."

"Nice that *some people* noticed."

His eyes glittered in the dash lights, and there was a long moment of tense silence. When he spoke, his voice was a throaty rasp. "You think I didn't notice?"

Jenny wasn't sure how to answer that. If he'd noticed, he'd done a darn good job of hiding it.

"You think I didn't notice?" he repeated, louder this time, crowding her.

Was the car getting smaller?

"You didn't say anything," she pointed out, fighting the urge to shrink back against the door.

"What, exactly, was it that you wanted me to say?" He leaned closer still, and a few beats of silence ticked past. "That your eyes look like emeralds without your glasses? That you have unbelievably sexy legs? That you should show off more often, by the way."

The front of his shoulder brushed the tip of hers, and Jenny swallowed against the electric sensation that passed between them.

His voice went lower. "That those shoes were designed to keep a man awake at night? That I've been watching the wisp of your hair, curling over your temple and resisting the urge to smooth it back all night long?"

Jenny couldn't move. She couldn't breathe. Her chest was frozen in place, while her pulse tripped over itself.

His fingertips fluttered against her temple, touching her hair. "Or that your red lips look soft, smooth, delicious?" His hand eased around to the back of her head, fingers splaying into her hair, as he drew her forward, his mouth coming down on hers in slow motion.

What was happening? What was going—

And then he was kissing her.

He was *kissing* her.

Sparks flew out from every corner of her body. Her skin prickled hot in the sultry car. Her belly buzzed and her thighs twitched, and her body leaned subconsciously toward him.

He parted his lips, deepening the kiss. His free arm slid around her waist, pulling her tight to his chest, while his tongue tested the seam of her lips.

She opened for him, and he invaded, spreading new waves of desire throughout her body. She whimpered, grasping his broad shoulders through his jacket for support while her world tipped on its axis.

He finally broke the kiss, touching his forehead gently against hers. "I noticed," he breathed.

With her brain struggling to grasp the enormity of what had just happened, "Oh," was all she managed.

He let her go, leaning back in his seat, closing his eyes for a long moment. "Sorry about that."

"It's, uh…" She straightened her dress again, sitting back in her own seat. "Fine," she ended.

It was more than fine. It had been amazing.

He'd noticed. He'd *noticed.* And he'd kissed her.

Wow, had he ever kissed her. She'd never been kissed like that in her life.

Mitch let off the emergency brake and put the Corvette in gear.

He pulled onto the gravel road and continued toward Jenny's small house beside Frost Lake.

She hadn't the first idea of what to say or do.

Mitch pulled his Corvette into Jenny's short driveway, his brain a jumble of lust and recrimination as he automatically turned off the headlights and killed the engine. He pushed open his door and rounded the hood to open hers.

In the ten minutes since he'd kissed her, neither of them had said a word. But inside his head, he'd given himself about a dozen stern lectures. What the hell did he think he was doing? Jenny was a nice girl, a great girl, a wonderful girl, and she worked for him.

She wasn't one of the sophisticated women he met at parties in New York and L.A., who wanted nothing more than a famous football player as a companion for the evening or the night. She was honest, uncomplicated, and he was a cad for giving in to his baser instincts.

He pulled open her door, forcing himself to concentrate on the treetops, the full moon hanging on the horizon and the darkened outline of her little house—anything, anything but looking at Jenny again.

He knew he should get the heck out of here without delay, but her porch light was out, and the gentleman in him wouldn't send her up the uneven pathway and the dark stairs on her own. He offered his arm, ignoring her light touch, looking straight ahead as they made their way along the stepping stones in her front garden.

They walked up the stairs and across the porch, then she stopped and turned toward him.

"I'm—" she began, and he made the mistake of meeting her gaze.

Her eyes were opaque jade in the faint moonlight, her lips red and swollen from his kiss. Her hair was disheveled, her cleavage highlighted by the sexy dress and those legs went on forever, ending in those fantasy shoes that somehow hijacked his primal brain. He groaned in instant surrender and swooped in for another kiss.

She tipped her head to accommodate him, soft lips parting, tongue answering his own, even as her slim arms wound around his neck. He wrapped his own arms around her narrow waist and pulled her against him once more, those luscious breasts flush to his chest. Her mouth was hot on his, her thighs taut, the feel of them hardening his body beyond imagination. He stroked a hand over her messy hair, releasing the clip that held it back, so that it tumbled free.

He kissed her temple, her ear, her neck, making his way along her bare shoulder.

"Mitch," she gasped, her breath hot puffs against his chest.

He drew back, looking into her soft green eyes. Her cheeks were flushed, her lips parted, and her shiny strawberry blond hair framed her face like a halo.

Walk away, he ordered himself. *Walk the hell away.*

But she pressed a key into his palm.

On automatic pilot, he unlatched the door, pushing it wide. He scooped her into his arms and carried her inside, slamming the door firmly behind them and making his way straight down the back hallway to her bedroom.

There, he lowered her gently to her feet.

"Jenny," he breathed, reminding himself of who this was, trying one more time to convince himself to do the right thing.

But she came up on her toes and kissed him passionately, and he'd spent far too many years being self-indulgent to summon self-discipline now. His hand moved reflexively to her breast, grasping the soft mound beneath the silky dress. She parted his suit jacket, her small hands sliding around his back, their heat searing through the thin cotton of his shirt.

He shrugged out of the jacket, and it fell to the floor. One of his thighs pressed between hers, easing her dress out of the way. She gasped, as the fabric of his slacks obviously hit home. Her hands fumbled with his tie, and he gave into temptation, slipping the single shoulder of the dress down her arm.

Their movements grew faster, more frantic.

She popped the buttons of his shirt, while he found the zipper at the back of her dress. In seconds, they were chest to chest, skin to skin, and he pressed long, deep, fiery kisses on her mouth.

Her dress slipped to the floor. Her scant panties combined with those shoes nearly sent him over the edge. He stripped off the remainder of his clothes and eased her down on the big bed, into the neatly pressed quilt and the plump, perfect pillows.

She was all motion beneath him, heat, softness, kisses and breathy cries. Her fingernails dug into his back, while he kissed her lips, her neck, her breasts, kneading his hands along her thighs, up and around. Impatiently, he tore off her panties. She gasped, then moaned and arched against his fingers.

He kissed her hard and deep, strumming her nipples. Her hands roamed his body. He shifted over her, and her legs wrapped around him, her hips arched against his weight in an invitation he couldn't ignore.

He grabbed for his slacks, quickly retrieving a condom before instinct obliterated reason. He thrust into her exquisite heat, his primal brain telling him to make it last and last and last. Pillows flew to the floor. The bed rocked on its brass foundation, while the stars through her bedroom window melted and slid from the sky.

She cried his name just as his own passion crested. His breathing went hoarse, and long minutes throbbed past before sanity returned. Exhausted, he rolled to his side, taking him with her, pulling her deep into his arms.

Once again, words eluded him. He had absolutely no idea what to say to her. He wasn't sorry. He didn't regret it. But, oh boy, had he ever made a big mistake.

Instead of speaking, he cradled her against his body, held her close until she was safely asleep. Then he held her an hour longer. He knew he'd be facing the stupidity of his actions full-on in the morning, but he was in no hurry to get there.

It wasn't until the moon was high in the sky, and Mitch knew he was in real danger of falling asleep right there next to Jenny, that he eased her from his arms and tucked the covers around her. He risked a gentle kiss at her hairline, before slipping into his clothes and leaving her sleeping.

Jenny wasn't surprised to wake up alone in the morning. Since the wedding had taken place on the holiday Monday, her alarm went off as usual for the workday on Tuesday. She had a few unfamiliar aches and pains in the shower, but she didn't mind. Mitch had noticed her. Boy, had he noticed her.

She was a little embarrassed about tumbling into bed with him so quickly. But it wasn't as though they were strangers. They were both adults, and he'd spent years living in big cities and moving in sophisticated social circles. She knew it was an entirely different dating world out there.

She dressed neatly and professionally for the office, her

glasses back in place, and took a cab to the TCC. She'd call the auto club and get a boost sometime during the morning.

As usual, she arrived before Mitch. She put on the coffee in their three-room, second-floor office area, booted up her computer, checked both her and Mitch's voice mail boxes for weekend messages and pulled her pending files out of the locked cabinet, sorting the issues in priority order on her desktop.

She was halfway through her new emails, when the door opened. She felt an excited hitch in her stomach and looked up to see Mitch walk into the office. A reflexive smile formed on her face. Should she stand? Would he hug her this morning? Kiss her? Or would they leave that kind of behavior outside the office?

He clicked the door shut. And when he turned back, she was surprised to see him scowling. Her smile drooped.

"Good morning," she offered, studying his expression. Was something wrong? Was there a problem she hadn't heard about? The rivalry over the upcoming club presidency election was well known. Had something more happened between Abigail and Brad?

Crisply dressed in his usual business suit, he set his jaw, squared his shoulders and crossed toward her.

She stood. "Mitch?"

"I owe you an apology," he began without preamble, his focus settling somewhere beyond her left ear.

"You don't—"

"My behavior last night was completely unforgivable."

What did he mean? That he hadn't danced with her, complimented her at the reception or that he'd left in the middle of the night without a word? Whichever it was, he was already forgiven.

"I took advantage of you, and I am profoundly sorry."

Now she was completely confused. Was he talking about their lovemaking? Because she had been as willing and eager as him.

"I stepped way out of line," Mitch continued, still not looking her in the eye. "You deserve better than that. You deserve better than me."

Wait a minute. She didn't want better than Mitch. She wanted Mitch.

He finally flicked a glance directly at her. "I hope you'll still be comfortable working here. I'll do everything in my power to make sure our professional relationship is not impacted." His dark eyes softened slightly. "Can you forgive me, Jenny? Can we possibly forget it ever happened?"

A lead weight pressed down on Jenny's chest, and her knees nearly buckled from lack of breath. Forget it ever happened? He wanted to forget he'd made love with her? Go on as if everything was normal, as if she was…was…some kind of one-night stand?

Reality washed over her like ice water.

She was a one-night stand.

Mitch had thought she was pretty, sexy, desirable and available last night, period. The sophisticated dress, heavy makeup and fancy hairdo hadn't given him romantic thoughts. They had given him lustful thoughts.

A clipped laugh of embarrassment slipped out, and she quickly covered her lips with her fingers.

What a fool she'd been.

His gaze narrowed. "Jenny?"

She scrambled to gather her emotions. This was one of those moments. She'd been stupid. She'd made a complete fool of herself. In the aftermath, she could pull it together and pretend she was as sophisticated and aloof as him, or she could break down altogether, and he'd remember forever that she behaved like a gauche teenager the morning after.

She wouldn't let that happen. She was tough. She was controlled. She could do this.

"No problem," she managed to assure him with a dismissive wave of her hand, sitting down and turning back to her computer. "Business as usual. I get it. We slipped up. Hey, it happens."

"Are you sure—"

"I'm fine," she said with forced brightness. "If you don't mind, I'd really like to get through these emails before coffee. The auto club will be here—" She stopped right there. No point in bringing up any reminders of their one-night fling. It was over and done, and she wasn't going to think about it ever again.

The desk phone rang, and she scooped it up, turning her back completely on Mitch. "Texas Cattleman's Club."

"What happened?" It was Emily's voice.

A flush prickled Jenny's scalp. "Can I call you back?"

"Is he there?"

"Yes."

"Roger. Got it. Call me back as soon as you can, okay?"

"I will." Just as soon as she went to the bathroom and threw up.

She hung up the phone and stared at her computer, the characters blurring in front of her eyes.

He was still standing behind her.

She could feel his heat and hear his breathing.

She schooled her features and turned. "Is there anything else?"

He looked lost, and a little confused—an unheard of state for Mitch Hayward. "I really am sorry."

Jenny gathered every bit of dignity she could muster. "So you said."

"Maybe we could—"

"I don't think talking about it is going to help."

He paused for a moment. "Right. I guess not."

"Like you said." She turned and punched a couple of random computer keys. "We'll simply forget it ever happened. Carry on as usual." And she was absolutely, positively going to date other men. This silly fantasy of hers had gone on far too long. She was nearly thirty. Mitch was nowhere in her future, and she was ready to fully accept that reality.

* * *

When Jenny finally left the office at the end of the workday, Emily was there in the parking lot, leaning up against Jenny's car, looking very impatient. Jenny's steps faltered, but she knew she couldn't avoid Emily forever.

"You didn't call me back," Emily accused, straightening away from the door panel.

"You sabotaged my car," Jenny pointed out. The auto club guy had boosted it midmorning, and the battery was back in shape now.

"For a good cause." Emily peered at Jenny's expression. "Seriously. What on earth happened last night?"

"My life's not going to change, that's for sure." Jenny focused on unlocking the car door.

"Did he insult you? Ignore you? What?"

Though she'd like nothing better than to take Mitch's advice and forget last night ever happened, Jenny knew she couldn't keep a secret like that from her best friend. It was too big, too devastating. It would eat her alive if she didn't share it. Though it might eat her alive even if she did.

"Get in," she told Emily, hitting the unlock button for the passenger side.

Emily quickly rounded the car and hopped in, pulling her seat belt into place. "Spill."

Jenny cranked the engine, putting the car into Reverse, swinging around to head for the parking lot exit. She needed to get clear of the TCC building and the feeling of having Mitch close by before she spoke.

She followed the curve of the road and put her mouth on automatic pilot, struggling to stay detached from the words she was uttering. She tried to pretend she was talking about someone else, some poor, hapless woman who'd let her emotions rule her logic and who got exactly what she'd deserved.

"At first," she told Emily, "it seemed like he didn't notice me at all. Nothing was different. Except he didn't ask me to dance.

He always asks me to dance. As if he has to. Like it's his duty. Since I'm technically his 'date.'"

"Jen? You're babbling."

"Right." Jenny's moist hands slipped on the warm steering wheel. "He didn't ask me to dance."

"I got that."

"I got ticked off and left. I mean, the hair, the dress, the makeup, the *shoes.* Do you blame me for being upset? Don't you think any normal, red-blooded guy would have asked me to dance?"

"I don't blame you for getting ticked off. And, for what it's worth, I thought you looked hot."

"Thank you. I agree. I felt like a fool. But I looked hot."

Emily smirked and snorted out a laugh.

"So, I leave the reception. I head for my car."

"Which I'd incapacitated."

Jenny nodded her acknowledgment. "Which you'd incapacitated. Thank you *very* much, by the way."

"Did it work?"

"Like a charm."

"I knew it would."

"He drove me home."

"I knew he would."

"And I slept with him."

"I knew—" Emily twisted in her seat. "Wait a minute. *What?*"

"I slept with Mitch." Jenny was really quite proud of how detached she sounded as she went into the sordid details. "I tore off my clothes. Or maybe I tore off his clothes, I can't quite remember the details. In any event, we were both naked."

Emily's voice rose to a squeal. "You *slept* with Mitch Hayward?"

Jenny glanced at her friend's incredulous expression. "Am I not saying this right?"

"On the first date?"

"Well, technically, it wasn't a date. Or I guess you could say it was our twelfth date, if you count dates that aren't really dates. But, really, at this point, I'm planning to take credit for them all. It makes me seem less slutty, don't you think?"

"You're not slutty."

"I slept with a guy on the first date."

"Twelfth date. And I thought you said your life wasn't going to change?"

Jenny missed a stop sign and sucked in a shocked breath when she realized what she'd done. She was a careful, conscientious driver. Fortunately for her, there was no cross traffic.

"Maybe you better pull over," Emily suggested in a worried tone.

"Yeah," Jenny agreed. She eased her car into the gravel parking lot of the Royal Diner. She kept a death grip on the steering wheel until she came to a complete stop.

"What happened?" Emily asked gently. When Jenny didn't answer, she put a comforting hand on her shoulder. "Jen?"

"This morning…" Jenny swallowed. She wasn't going to cry. She was an adult, and she would not cry over a cad like Mitch. "When he got to the office. He told me he was sorry, and he hoped we could forget all about it, carry on as usual, as if nothing had happened."

"I can't imagine Mitch—seriously?"

"Yes."

"Did he say anything else?"

"That I deserved better than him."

It was Emily's turn to go silent. They both reflexively watched while a car pulled past them and turned into a spot near the diner's front door. The car doors opened, and two teenagers hopped out.

Jenny was pretty sure she knew what Emily was thinking. It was what Jenny was thinking. It was what any reasonably intelligent adult would conclude.

"Yeah," she voiced it out loud, her tone mocking. "He gave me the old, 'it's not you, it's me, babe' brush-off."

"Ouch," Emily whispered.

"I can't believe I was a one-night stand. I'd have bet money against that ever happening. To me of all people. I'm not stupid, Em."

"Of course you're not stupid," Emily staunchly defended. "I never would have guessed that Mitch of all people—"

"He's a football star," Jenny reminded her, feeling defeated. She wished she'd remembered that important fact last night. "He's a celebrity, and the world is his oyster. I bet he does this kind of thing all the time."

"But not with you."

"He has now."

Emily gestured with a spread palm. "But, you're not... You know."

"I am now."

Emily thwacked her head against the seatback. "This is ridiculous."

"I'm over it."

"You are not."

"I am. I have no choice. What you told me last night was spot-on. And I promised myself if this didn't work out, I'd date other men. That's exactly what I'm going to do. Pining away over Mitch Hayward has gotten me exactly nowhere in the past, and it will get me exactly nowhere in the future. I *refuse* to do something so illogical."

Emily sat up straighter, eyes narrowing, forehead creasing. "Are you serious?"

"Absolutely." Jenny had never been more serious in her life.

Emily smacked the dashboard. "Then let's get going."

"Where?"

"Take Bainbridge to Payton for Harper's Boutique. You're going to need a new wardrobe."

Three

After an excruciatingly long day at work, followed by a grueling physiotherapy session for his injured shoulder, Mitch pulled his Corvette in front of the garage of his rented, split-level house. The pain in his shoulder was bad enough, but then there were some of Jenny's words that he couldn't seem to get out of his mind.

"We slipped up," she'd said. "Hey, it happens." As if it was the kind of thing that had happened to her in the past. As if anything like their lovemaking had *ever* happened to him.

Sure, he'd dated his share of women. He was on the road, in the public eye, invited to parties and publicity events where supermodels wanted to hobnob with athletes.

But it wasn't the same thing. There had never been anything like his night—well, his half night—with Jenny.

He exited the cool car, using his left arm to push the door shut, cursing the fact that his shoulder wasn't healing as quickly as he'd hoped. He knew he wasn't eighteen anymore, but he was in top physical shape, and he'd done every single thing the doctors and physiotherapists had told him to do.

He heard the sound of footsteps and looked up to see Cole, who lived across the street, pacing his way down the driveway.

"Hey," Cole greeted with a nod, striding forward. Living so close to one another, the two men spent many casual evenings in each other's company.

"Hey," Mitch returned, hitting the lock button on his key fob. "Shoulder okay?"

"It will be. But my physio is a sadist."

"Poor baby."

Mitch grunted.

"Got a beer?" asked Cole.

"Sure," Mitch answered as he started for the front door. He'd rather have a double shot of single malt. But he'd read studies that told him drinking alcohol to relieve pain was a dangerous path to start down. He wondered if it was as dangerous for emotional pain as it was for physical pain.

"You took Jenny home last night," Cole stated as he followed behind.

"So?" Mitch's tone came out uncharacteristically sharp. But the last thing he wanted to do was talk about Jenny. "Her car broke down."

"I saw she left it in the TCC parking lot."

Case closed. There was nothing unusual about Mitch offering Jenny a ride home. He didn't owe anybody any explanation.

He inserted his key and swung open the front door. He retrieved his *Royal Crier* newspaper from the metal bracket beside his house, and grabbed a handful of mail from his mailbox. Then he tossed it all, along with the keys, onto the side table in his small foyer.

The house was cool and dark, and he breathed a sigh of relief at being home. Maybe he'd take some pain pills later tonight. He had a feeling it was going to be a challenge to get to sleep.

"I was on the phone with Abigail for an hour today," he told

Cole, changing the subject from Jenny and choosing something familiar and safe as he crossed the living room to open the blinds. The direct sunlight had passed over his house hours ago and would now be shining on the back deck.

"Does she know that Brad's being threatened with blackmail?" Cole asked. Few people knew about the blackmail threats to Brad, but Cole was a trusted confidant of most TCC board members and had been brought into the loop.

Mitch shook his head. "Not yet. At least not that she mentioned. She has some strong opinions on the design for the new clubhouse."

Brad and Abigail were locked in a bitter fight for the upcoming presidential election at the Texas Cattleman's Club. Mitch was pretty sure that Abigail would have spoken up if she knew that Brad was receiving vague, threatening notes that talked about exposing his "secret."

"Whatever it is, it's going to come out sooner or later."

"I'm betting sooner." Mitch opened the refrigerator and snagged two icy cold imported beers. "That's the thing about secrets."

"That's the thing about secrets," said Cole, an oblique look in his eyes as he accepted one of the chilled, green bottles. He twisted off the cap and tossed it into the trash.

Ignoring Cole's dire tone, Mitch opened his own bottle and headed for the back deck. He settled into a padded chair beneath the shade of the awning, propping up his right arm to relieve the stress on his shoulder.

The deck provided a view across the seventh green of the Royal Golf Club. Two men were putting in the distance, while a foursome, two men and two women, made their way to the eighth tee. A breeze rippled the leaves on the perimeter oaks, bringing with it the scent of freshly cut grass.

Cole sat down. "Secrets," he said, then took a swig.

"You got one that matters?" asked Mitch, trying to gauge his friend's expression.

Cole smiled. "I think you do."

Mitch squinted. "You know something I don't?" Most of his life had been splashed across the national tabloids. Everybody in the country knew his yardage, his college grades, his weight. They'd even done a spread on his new haircut last fall.

"You got home at 4:00 a.m."

Mitch stilled, and his voice lowered to a warning growl. He did not need to defend himself to Cole. "Last time I checked, I was over twenty-one."

"You were with Jenny." Cole's tone wasn't exactly judgmental, but there was a steadiness in his eyes that made Mitch feel like he was under interrogation.

Mitch didn't want to lie, but he wasn't about to tarnish Jenny's reputation, either. So, he didn't respond.

"Are you sure that was such a good idea?" asked Cole.

Mitch felt his heartbeat deepen, while adrenaline trickled into his system. "You might want to think about exiting this conversation along about now."

"I'm worried about Jenny."

"Jenny's fine."

"How would you know that?"

Mitch forced in a calming breath and took a long pull on his beer. He knew he should never have kissed her. And after she'd made his blood pressure skyrocket there in the car, he should never have walked her to the door.

But it was done. And he couldn't change it. And it was none of anybody else's damn business.

"What are your intentions?" ask Cole, his gaze steely.

"Is this a joke?"

"I'm dead serious. I've known Jenny since she was a little girl—"

"And I haven't?"

"I didn't sleep with her."

Mitch came instantly to his feet, pain throbbing through his shoulder. He hated mounting an argument when he was in the wrong. Oh, he could do it. But he sure hated it. "Jenny is an adult. We talked this morning and—"

"And she told you she was fine?" Cole asked, brow arched.

Mitch came clean. "She said 'we slipped up' and 'hey, it happens.'"

"Does that sound like Jenny to you?"

And that was where Mitch's logic fell off the rails. It didn't sound remotely like Jenny.

The accusation went out of Cole's eyes, and Mitch felt his guard slip a notch.

Both men were silent for a few minutes, while the wind picked up, and the golf games continued on the course.

"What were you *thinking?*" asked Cole.

Mitch eased back down in his seat. "You saw her last night."

"Yet I didn't sleep with her." Then Cole's gaze grew contemplative, as if he was questioning his own judgment on that front.

Something dark burst to life inside Mitch, and he reflexively jerked forward. "Don't you dare even think about sleeping with Jenny."

Cole looked amused now. He obviously saw some kind of twisted humor in Mitch's predicament. "That sounded a whole lot like jealousy. Why don't you tell me again how you have no intentions toward her?"

Mitch could tell where Cole was going. But there was absolutely no future for him and Jenny. Jenny was a great girl, and Mitch was only human. "You know what I'm like."

He and Cole had been friends since elementary school. Cole had played baseball instead of football, his smaller stature making that game a better fit. But he was fully aware of the perks available to elite athletes. And he was under no illusions about Mitch's lifestyle.

"You're not the guy I'd pick for my sister, that's for sure," Cole agreed.

"You don't have a sister."

"If I had one."

"I'll be leaving town after the election, or as soon as my shoulder heals," Mitch added to the discussion. There was absolutely no future for the two of them. And Jenny deserved a guy who could give her a future.

Nipping things in the bud was the only way to keep from hurting her even more.

"I talked with Jeffrey Porter last night," he put in, knowing it was a way to further emphasis his undesirability as a match for Jenny. Cole was well aware of Jeffrey's many indiscretions.

Cole lifted his beer bottle in a mock toast. "Is he serving as your cautionary tale?"

"His girlfriend caught him cheating. You know," Mitch mused aloud, "I honestly think Jeffrey said 'no' to the first hundred propositions. Then maybe one night he was alone. Maybe we'd lost the game. Maybe he got hurt on the field. Maybe the coach had reamed him out for something, and maybe he'd had a fight over the phone with Celeste. And there she was, a fresh, pretty, willing little sweet thing that would make all his problems go away. At least for a while. And so, he stumbled. And once he'd done it the first time, well…"

Mitch had watched the same scenario play out with dozens of players. His teammates tried to make relationships work, yet, inevitably, they were spectacular failures.

"You don't have to sell me on the general sleaziness of professional athletes," said Cole.

"I'm trying to sell you on the general sleaziness of *me*. I'm going back to that world, Cole. And I'm no different than any other guy on the team."

"Then you had no business sleeping with Jenny."

Mitch grunted out a cold laugh.

He ought to be drawn and quartered for what he'd done to Jenny. Guys like him had no business sniffing around caring, wholesome, defenseless girls like her.

* * *

Jenny was keeping a sinful secret. It had to do with her updated wardrobe. Though she'd worn her usual Friday outfit of gray linen slacks, matching blazer and her favorite aqua silk blouse to the office this morning, underneath it all, she wore skimpy purple lace panties and a matching push-up bra.

She and Emily had spent every evening this week shopping for new clothes. They'd started Tuesday at Harper's Boutique. Then, they'd moved on to every high-fashion store within a fifty-mile radius.

Even if nobody had a clue, Jenny felt a little bit sexy. It was good for her bruised ego. As Emily had said on the drive home last night, Mitch had no idea what he was missing.

The outer office door opened with a rattle, and a uniformed courier entered, a white cardboard envelope in one hand and his electronic tracking device in the other.

"Delivery for Mr. Hayward," the young man announced. He crossed the room and perched the envelope against her upright in-basket, holding out the tracking device.

Jenny took it and scrolled her signature across the grayed window. "Thanks."

"Have a good day." He gave her a salute of acknowledgment while he turned to leave.

As the door swung shut behind him, she ripped the perforated tab and reached into the depths of the cardboard pouch, extracting a smaller manila envelope. She retrieved a letter opener and sliced through the paper. Inside, she discovered four VIP tickets to tonight's football game in Houston. The Texas Tigers versus the Chicago Crushers.

Her mood slipped another notch.

Like any good Texan, she loved football. And the last three times Mitch had been sent complimentary tickets to a nearby game, he'd invited her to join the group. But those days were obviously over.

A folded note slipped out of the envelope, and she opened it up. *The jet will be at the airport at four,* it read. *Bring a date.* It was signed by Mitch's friend and teammate Jeffrey Porter.

"Jenny, can you please look up—" Mitch stopped short.

A jolt of guilt hit her. Which was ridiculous. She opened Mitch's mail all the time. There was nothing on this package to indicate it was personal. And it wasn't. He was a football player. He received packages from his team with some regularity.

"The tickets?" he asked, moving forward.

She nodded. Bundling them along with the note back into the manila envelope, pretending everything was perfectly normal in her world. "They say the jet will be at the airport at four." For a split second, she wondered who his date might be, but then she quickly cut off that line of thinking, mentally admonishing herself.

She rose to deposit the empty cardboard packaging into the recycling bin.

She heard Mitch behind her, the envelope rustling. He was clearly reading the enclosed note.

Determined to banish the annoying jealousy, she turned and moved briskly back to her chair.

But she no sooner sat down than perversity made her speak out. "So, who are you taking?"

He went still, and she had to fight the urge to glance at his expression. She focused on picking up the scattered bits of cardboard from the envelope tab. She rolled them between her fingers and tossed them in the wastebasket.

Then she straightened a stack of papers on her desk, returned her letter opener to the drawer and lined up three pens in front of her phone.

Mitch's voice was a deep rumble. "Do you want to come to the game, Jenny?"

She forced out a little laugh. "Of course not. That would be silly."

"You can join me if you'd like."

She looked up to where he stood above her, tone tart. "I would not like."

Her words dropped into silence.

His gaze held hers, and for a long moment she couldn't breathe. He seemed to be searching deep into her eyes.

Then his lips compressed, and his broad shoulders drew back beneath his suit. "You do understand why I'm no good for you, right?"

"Absolutely."

He was no good for her because there were hundreds of beautiful women out there who were perfectly willing to throw themselves at a star quarterback. And Mitch was a star quarterback who wanted to be in a position to catch them.

She was a fool to ever think she could hold his attention. She wasn't a movie star. She wasn't a supermodel. And she sure wasn't a bored debutante looking for a walk on the wild side.

"It has everything to do with me, and nothing to do with you," he said.

"You do know that's the oldest line in the book."

"In this case, it happens to be true."

"Well, that would be a first."

His eyes narrowed. "You've heard it before?"

"Not me, specifically," she admitted.

He snorted out a cold laugh. "Can we stop?"

"Sure." She turned to her computer, pretending to read an email while she waited for him to walk away.

"That's not what I meant," he finally said.

She didn't turn back. "Then what did you mean?"

"I'm inviting you to a football game."

"And I'm turning you down."

Mitch tapped the envelope against the desktop. "You're making way too much of this."

At that, she did turn. "You're the one who won't go away."

"Because you're being ridiculously stubborn. You love football. Come out and have some fun."

"I have plans with Emily tonight." They were going out manhunting, tonight and every Friday night until they found the right guys.

"Bring her along," Mitch countered.

"She doesn't like football."

"She likes private jets. And there'll be a VIP party after the game."

Jenny found herself hesitating. He was right about Emily liking the VIP world. In fact, she could almost hear Emily's voice now, extolling the virtues of a party chockablock with single male notables from the Houston area. A target-rich environment was how she'd describe it.

And Jenny did want Emily to find the right man. Emily's talk of getting pregnant while she was still single had Jenny worried. Single parenthood was a grueling struggle, and she wouldn't wish it on anyone.

It wasn't like she'd have to stick to Mitch's side, either at the game or at the party. In fact, she could mostly ignore him. It would be a big party, full of other guests.

"You and I won't be alone at all," Mitch assured her, breaking the silence.

The unexpected statement surprised a laugh out of Jenny. "Are you afraid I won't be able to keep my hands off you?"

"No." He didn't smile, and he didn't elaborate. His gaze remained steady on her eyes, and for some reason she thought he meant the opposite. But that was crazy. Sexy, famous Mitch could easily keep his hands off staid, plain Jenny.

Still, a buzz of awareness shimmied through her system, and she silently berated herself for the weakness. How long was it going to take for these ridiculous feelings to go away?

"Fifty-yard line," he added.

"You think that'll tempt me?"

"Yes, I do. Row four."

Okay, she was tempted. But she promised herself that it had nothing to do with spending time with Mitch. They were great seats. And it would be a great party. And she had four brand-new outfits to choose from.

Plus, she knew Emily would love the trip. Emily had been incredibly supportive and unbelievably patient all week long. The very least Jenny owed her was a target-rich VIP party.

An optimistic smile twitched Mitch's lips. "You'll be able to smell the sweat and hear the cuss words."

Jenny made up her mind. "Wow. What girl could say no to that?"

The Tigers won the game twenty-one to six, so the mood afterward at the Moberly Club party on Galveston Bay was celebratory. With Emily's wholehearted approval, Jenny had worn navy leggings and royal blue leather ankle boots, topped with a flirty denim miniskirt and a shimmering peach tank top. They'd done the makeup thing again, put in her contacts and pulled her hair back in a messy knot, topping the whole outfit off with dangling silver earrings.

Jenny wasn't used to men's interested gazes following her progress while she crossed a room. But she steeled herself, squared her shoulders and ordered herself to relax and have a good time. There was a dance band playing in the corner. She'd ordered a bright-colored cranberry martini and took a first sip. When Cole Maddison asked her to dance, she accepted cheerfully and slid off the bar stool.

The club had been closed for the team's private party, and everyone seemed to know everyone else. Most of the players were built for strength and not agility, so the dancing caliber was mixed. Their laughing efforts made Jenny relax, and she gave herself over to the music.

Across from her, Cole did the same. He was under six feet, and much slighter than all the other men around him. But his movements were smooth and practiced. His smile was broad. And she felt emotionally safe in his company.

"May I cut in?" came a deep voice at her side.

Jenny glanced up to see Jeffrey Porter's bright smile. She'd met him a few times over the years, and she knew he was a good friend of Mitch's.

She looked to Cole, who shrugged his shoulders and raised his palms, backing away to the beat of the band.

Jeffrey wore a white cotton dress shirt and black jeans. His skin was olive-toned, and his jet-black hair was pulled back in a ponytail at the base of his neck. In her experience, he was invariably friendly and jovial. All the other players seemed to like him.

The band switched to a slower number, and he drew her into his massive arms. "We should take this nice and slow," he spoke in her ear. "I'm not the most graceful guy on the floor."

"No spins or dips?" she teased.

"It's for your own safety, ma'am."

She laughed. "Nice catch out there, by the way." She referred to a late game play in the end zone where Jeffrey had leaped a good five feet to snag the ball and score a touchdown before smacking into the turf.

"Thank you. Mitch would have drilled it straight to me, saved me a bruise or two."

"You think?"

"Don't get me wrong. Cooper's a decent quarterback. But Mitch is psychic."

Jenny drew back. "Psychic?"

"Yes, ma'am."

"Does he ever give you any stock tips?"

It was Jeffrey's turn to laugh, and his brown eyes crinkled up at the corners. "Wouldn't that be something?"

"My 401(k) could sure use the help." Jenny spotted Emily across the dance floor in Cole's arms. In her ultrahigh heels, they were nearly nose to nose. Her expression looked tense, her movements stiff, and Jenny couldn't help but wonder what was wrong.

"My salary's just fine," said Jeffrey. "But I expect my career to be short."

Jenny's attention went back to Jeffrey. "You do? Is something wrong?"

"I'm going by the mathematical odds. It's tough out there."

Jenny cringed reflexively in sympathy, remembering some of the hits Jeffrey had received in the game. She leaned in. "Are you in pain?"

"I'm always in pain. But that's not the same as being injured." He nodded toward the perimeter tables. "Now, Mitch there. He's injured. And his physiotherapy regime is brutal."

Jenny glanced sideways to where Mitch stood in a group of other players. He gazed intently at her, with what looked like anger simmering in his darkened eyes.

She missed a step, but Jeffrey quickly caught her, tugging her close. "Whoa, there, missy."

"Sorry," she breathed, refocusing her attention. What on earth was the matter with Mitch now?

Four

Mitch watched from the sidelines at the Moberly Club, while out on the dance floor Jeffrey flirted with Jenny. Though he knew she was too smart to be taken in by Jeffrey's smooth talk, he was tempted to warn her away from the man. Or maybe he should order Jeffrey to stay away from her. It might be his responsibility to make it clear, in no uncertain terms, that Jeffrey was to stay well away from his assistant.

He straightened away from bar, intending to do just that.

"Well, hello, stranger." A tall, leggy blonde sidled up to him.

"Misha," he greeted, recognizing the former wife of one of Houston's many oil executives. "I didn't know you were in town."

"Back from Paris last week," she purred, resting her elegant, manicured hand on the arm of his suit jacket. She was a former model, born and raised in Germany. She'd had a brief but profitable marriage in Houston. Word on the street was that he'd ended up with the sports cars, while she got the Tigers' season tickets.

"Would you care to dance?" he asked dutifully, even though he'd prefer to spend his time confronting Jeffrey.

"But, of course." She took his hand and moved to the dance floor.

Misha, it turned out, had spent the past few months traveling, perfecting her tan in Tahiti, visiting a game preserve in South Africa and dedicating a new museum wing in Prague. She offered to show him her all-over tan, but Mitch graciously declined.

His next dance partner was just back from St. Kitts. It seemed she'd bought a little bungalow beside the ocean. She'd taken up snorkeling. She throatily informed him there was a hot tub on the balcony of her hotel suite, and then hinted that she'd like to show him how long she could hold her breath.

Mitch honestly didn't remember these parties being quite so crass. By midnight, all he wanted to do was head for the hotel, take an aspirin and crawl under the covers.

Alone.

But then his gaze caught Jenny.

She was in the corner talking to Emily, being handed another martini. A green one this time. She seemed to have developed a taste for exotic drinks. And he didn't know what had gotten into her with the clothes lately.

That short skirt showed off her incredible legs, and their navy silhouette made a man's mind go all kinds of places. She'd worn her contacts again, and her ornate earrings sparkled whenever she moved her head. His gaze rested on the shimmering peach tank top, making out the rounded curves of her breasts against the slinky fabric. It was obvious she'd forgone a bra.

He couldn't remember ever seeing her braless. Then again, he supposed he hadn't been looking. Why was he looking now? What the hell was the matter with him? What, exactly, would it take for him to learn his lesson?

He caught sight of Jeffrey. The man was heading in Jenny's

direction again, a predatory gleam in his eyes. This time, Mitch did make his move. And he didn't let anyone stop him along the way.

"Jeffrey," he greeted heartily, falling into step with the man.

"Hey, Mitch. Glad you could make it."

Mitch would just bet Jeffrey was glad he'd shown up with Jenny. "I see you've met Jenny."

Jeffrey frowned. "I've met her lots of times before."

"You didn't dance with her before."

"Her hotness factor's gone way up in my books."

"You keep her out of your books."

Jeffrey turned his head to look at Mitch. "Huh? What are you talking about?"

"She's my assistant, you moron. Keep your hands off her."

"We were only dancing."

Mitch shot Jeffrey a dark look. "You're talking to me here, Jeff."

Jeffrey gave a sheepish smile. "Point taken."

"She's a nice girl."

"Then she'll slap me across the face, won't she?"

"You give her any reason to slap you across the face, and your face will be meeting up with my fist."

Jeffrey sputtered out a laugh. "So says the cripple."

"I've still got my left."

In answer, Jeffrey looped an arm over Mitch's shoulder. "Careful, buddy. You're starting to sound territorial."

"I told you, she's my assistant."

"And that's all she is?"

"Absolutely." If Mitch said it out loud often enough, maybe it would come true.

"Why don't I believe you?"

Probably because Mitch was lying. "Because your brain's in the gutter."

"Your brain and mine have been partying together down there for quite a few years."

Mitch spoke slowly and deliberately. "Not with Jenny."

"Hey, Jenny," Jeffrey sang out as they approached. He did a few mock dance steps, making her smile. "Got time for one more spin around the floor?"

Jenny turned and stumbled ever so slightly on her high-heeled boots, bracing herself against the bar. Her green eyes were bright, her smile more dazzling than usual. Mitch had seen her with only the two, but how many drinks had she had?

"We have to head out," Mitch interrupted before she could answer. If there was any chance her judgment was clouded, Jeffrey was the last guy she needed to be around.

"It's barely midnight," Jeffrey protested.

"We've planned an early flight in the morning," Mitch lied again. They could take the jet back to Royal anytime they wanted. But he stepped up beside Jenny, threading her arm through his.

"Cole around?" he asked Emily.

The woman sniffed her delicate nose. "How would I know?"

"You were dancing with him."

"Only till I could get rid of him."

Jenny pointed. "Over there. Behind the pillar." She started to move, but Mitch held on, causing her to trip again.

"How many martinis did you drink?" he asked.

She looked up at him, blinking her long lashes as if to bring him into focus. "I ordered two. But I barely sipped either of them. Why?"

"Because you're a lightweight," he murmured.

"Thank you." She nodded sarcastically. "I just lost three pounds."

He couldn't stop a grin at her joke as he ushered her forward to where they could meet up with Cole. "Time for bed, princess."

As they passed Jeffrey, the man shook his head, chuckling darkly at Mitch. "Assistant. Right."

Mitch threw a surreptitious elbow into Jeffrey's rib cage.

* * *

"I'm starving," said Jenny from the third-row seat in the chauffeur-driven Escalade as they sped along the shore of Galveston Bay.

Mitch twisted his head to look at her. "That's probably a good idea. A little food in your stomach along with the liquor."

"Will you stop," Jenny huffed. "I sipped on two teeny little martinis. I'm just hungry because it's late. Look." She pointed out the tinted window, turning her head as they cruised past the red neon sign. "Cara Mia Trattoria. And it's open."

Cole spoke up from the bucket seat next to Mitch's in the middle row. "If she can read Italian, she can't be that bad off."

Jenny smacked the back of Cole's bucket seat. "I'm perfectly sober, people."

Cole grinned, while Emily gave a shrug. "I could eat."

Mitch turned forward to address the driver. "Can you take us back to Cara Mia?"

"Of course, sir," the uniformed man responded. He checked the rearview mirror, then pulled a U-turn in advance of an upcoming red light, taking up the right-hand lane, before signaling to pull up to Cara Mia's front door.

As the SUV came to a smooth halt, Mitch handed the man a twenty-dollar tip.

"Thank you, sir. You have the service's number?"

"I do," Mitch confirmed, yawning the door open.

"We're on duty for the team until three."

Mitch nodded his thanks and stepped out of the vehicle. He turned to offer his hand to Emily, who'd been sitting behind him, but his gaze moved reflexively to Jenny's flirty skirt as she exited from Cole's side.

"They have a deck," she announced as she rounded the back of the SUV. Wisps of hair had worked loose from her knot and curled enchantingly around her bright face. "Do you think we can sit out there?"

Mitch curled her arm around his own, steadying her across

the cobblestone drive. "I'm sure they'll let us sit wherever we want."

She inhaled. "I love the ocean."

Wind bent the palm leaves, and rolling waves sounded rhythmically in the distance.

"Fresh air's probably good for you," he observed while she disentangled her arm from his and stepped toward the restaurant stairs.

The hostess wove her way in front of them through the crowded tables on the restaurant's deck. She showed them to a view table, overlooking lighted gardens, an expansive lawn and stone walkways that led down to a sandy beach. The tide was in, and the surf was up. Propane heaters warmed the air, and a floral centerpiece anchored the billowing white cloth on the round table.

Jenny plunked into a padded wicker chair and snagged a leather-bound menu.

A waiter filled their water glasses and offered cocktails, but they all opted for iced tea.

"Isn't that gorgeous?" Jenny's attention was distracted by the tiny pink lights decorating the flower gardens. In an instant, she was on her feet, crossing to the rail of the sundeck for a better look.

"Chicken marsala pizza?" suggested Cole. "With avocado and eggplant."

Emily peered over her menu at him. "What is that? Like, nerd pizza?"

"Are you calling me a nerd?"

She smirked. "Just commenting on your taste in pizza."

"Well, what do you suggest?"

"Sausage, ham, peppers, mushrooms, onions, pepperoni."

"What are you, pledging a fraternity?"

"It's a classic."

"You want me to order a pitcher of draft to go with it?" asked Cole. "We could have a chugging contest."

Emily stuck out her tongue at him.

Mitch chuckled low at the pair's antics, glancing to check out Jenny at the rail of the deck.

She was gone.

He straightened in his chair, gaze darting from table to table. Had she gone to the ladies' room?

He stood.

"What?" Emily asked.

"Where's Jenny?"

Emily and Cole peered around the busy deck.

Mitch's gaze snagged on her boots, discarded beneath her chair at the table. He instantly shifted his attention to the lighted gardens. There she was, halfway down the stone path, meandering her way toward the ocean.

"Got her." He pointed, tossing his napkin onto the table. "I'll be right back."

He trotted down the stairs and strode his way through the quiet gardens toward the beach. The salt tang grew stronger, and the roar of the waves filled his ears as he caught up to Jenny.

"Going somewhere?" he asked as her feet hit the sand.

"Just breathing the night air," she responded, and turned in a circle.

"Only two drinks?" he confirmed.

She shook her head and rolled her eyes.

"I was afraid you'd decided to take a swim," he admitted.

"It'll take more than a few sips of a martini to get me into the ocean in September." She plunked down on the soft sand.

Once again, he was struck by how different she seemed from the regular Jenny who masterminded his financial spreadsheets, deftly handled demanding club members and wrote concise, informative month-end reports. The transformation was more than a little disconcerting.

He eased down beside her, taking in her little skirt spread out in the sand. The shimmering top left most of her tanned back bare, while her breasts pressed teasingly against the thin fabric, nipples pebbled in the cool air.

"Interesting outfits you've been choosing lately," he heard himself observe, dragging his gaze away from her sexiness.

"I needed a new look," she told him, nodding out to sea. "If I want to snag a man."

Something hitched in Mitch's stomach. "You want to find a man?"

"Of course I want to find a man. All women want to find a man." She turned back to him and pointed her index finger for emphasis. "And if they tell you they don't, well… Well, maybe they don't. But most of them do. And I do."

Her eyes were round and soft in the glow from the gardens. Her cheeks were flushed, and her lips were pursed in a determined little moue that he wanted so badly to kiss. He gritted his teeth against the unruly urge, his stomach tightening.

"You had them lining up at the Moberly Club," he pointed out. "You must have danced with Jeffrey five times."

"Jeffrey's nice," she sighed.

Mitch felt his gut clench tighter. He needed to nip this Jeffrey fixation in the bud. "Jeffrey's not a good guy for you."

"I'm not that crazy about his ponytail."

"Well. Good." Not that the ponytail was the biggest worry by any stretch of the imagination.

"Jeffrey likes you a lot." She smoothed out a patch of sand with her palm, then traced her fingertips in a pattern through it.

At the moment, Mitch couldn't say he was exactly returning the favor. What if Jeffrey decided to cut his ponytail? Mitch would cut off a ponytail. For the right woman.

Wait a minute. What was he saying? There was no right woman. There were only women. Plural. Sophisticated and uncomplicated, and in keeping with his pro-football lifestyle.

Jenny smoothed out the sandy patch again, then drew a big heart with her index finger.

Mitch found himself waiting for her to draw initials.

"Jeffrey says you're psychic," she put in instead.

Mitch glanced up. "He what?"

"He told me you were psychic." She pushed the sand off her hand and held it out to him, palm up. "Go ahead. Read my future." She came to her knees looking decidedly earnest. "Tell me about the tall, dark, handsome dream man I'm going to marry. I'd like two kids, a white picket fence. And throw in a dog, will you?"

He took her hand, realizing it was just an excuse to touch her, but not particularly caring.

She looked so sweet in the dappled light.

"What kind of dog?" he asked, pretending to take her seriously.

"A Dalmatian."

"Isn't that a little big?"

She gazed up at him. "This isn't how it's supposed to work. You tell me what kind of dog."

"Oh. All right." He obediently looked down at her outspread hand.

He gave in to the temptation to run the pad of his thumb over her palm, tracing the faint lines on her soft skin. "I predict a long and happy life."

"That's lame."

"I thought everybody wanted a long and happy life."

"You need to be more specific."

"Okay." He squinted. "Here we go. Next Tuesday." He paused. "You're going to buy a purple dress."

She tipped her head, peering closer. "Will it help me snag a man?"

"Tall, dark and handsome," he put in, ignoring the jolt of emotion at the thought of her on a honeymoon with some random stranger. It was bad enough watching her dance with Jeffrey.

A serene smile grew on her face. "That sounds nice."

Mitch found he didn't like her reaction, not one little bit. "Wait a minute," he elaborated. "He cheats on you and you kick him to the curb."

"What? No. No way."

Mitch shrugged. "Afraid so."

"You're lying."

"I calls 'em as I sees 'em."

She tugged her hand away and gazed out across the bay. "You're a terrible fortune-teller."

He couldn't help but chuckle at her outrage. To make amends, he held out his own hand. "Here, you predict mine."

She didn't even bother to look at it. "You're going to die alone and lonely."

"What did I do to deserve that?" Not that he was denying it. It was most likely true.

"You're a heartbreaker, Mitch."

"Not on purpose." There had been a few women who'd expressed disappointment that he didn't want to get into a serious relationship. He'd always chalked it up to the fame and money factors. He knew he wasn't enough of a prize that a woman might actually miss him for himself.

"Result's the same," she told him. And she looked so dejected, that he found himself desperate to put the smile back on her face.

"How 'bout I make up for being such a cad," he teased. "I could get you a Dalmatian puppy. Or a kitten. Kittens are a lot less work."

She gave him a look of exasperation. "I don't want a pet."

She wanted a man. He got it. He hated it, but he got it. She wanted the kind of man Mitch would never be. He knew what he should say, knew what he had to say and what he had to do.

His tone was decisive. "I'll help you find one."

"A pet?"

"A man."

Jenny's eyes went wide. *"What?"*

"If you're sure that's what you want." His voice grew stronger.

"I'm here for you, Jenny. I know a lot of men. Jeffrey's a bad choice, but—"

She jumped to her feet, swiping the sand off the back of her denim skirt. "Have you lost your mind?"

He watched the strokes of her palms for a moment, but then quickly checked his wandering imagination. "I'm happy to help out," he lied, rising with her.

"You are *not* going to fix me up with your friends."

It certainly wasn't his first choice, but it was a perfectly practical approach to her problem. And to his. Since mooning after her like a lovesick adolescent wasn't getting him anywhere. "I don't see why not."

"Because it's insulting, for one."

"How is that insulting? I have nice friends. Most of them are physically fit. Most have money. Many of them are considered handsome."

"Read my lips." She stared up at him in the dim light.

His gaze went obediently to her mouth.

"No," she enunciated.

"Wow. Such a coherent and cohesive argument."

Her eyes crackled emerald. "Hell, no."

He couldn't help but grin.

"Mr. Hayward?" came a stranger's voice.

Mitch swiftly cut his attention to a cluster of teenage boys tentatively approaching across the sand.

"Is that you?"

Mitch inwardly sighed but mustered up a hearty professional smile for the teenagers. "It sure is."

There were five in all, maybe sixteen or seventeen years old. Barefoot, they wore knee-length, brightly colored shorts topped with an assortment of team T-shirts.

"Wow," one breathed, while a couple of the boys elbowed each other playfully.

"We play varsity for Gulfport Collegiate."

"Took State last year."

"I'm a quarterback, just like you."

Mitch widened his smile. "Congratulations," he offered to them collectively.

"Man, I wish we had something he could sign."

"I wish we had a ball."

The tallest jumped up and made a mock catch. "Mitch Hayward, right on the money."

His friends chuckled at their own cleverness.

"Except for Davey, here," one spoke up, taking the smallest of the group in a headlock.

The short boy struggled to get out.

"Davey doesn't play," said the tall one.

"Too puny," voiced another.

"One of my best friends is your size, Davey," Mitch offered, and the larger boy immediately let him go.

"He played baseball in high school." Mitch folded his arms across his chest. "But he spent most of his time in the computer lab. His software company now owns twenty percent of the Texas Tigers." Mitch's gaze took in the rest of the group. "You'll want to treat Davey with a little respect. One day, he might be signing your paychecks."

Davey grinned, while the rest of the boys sobered, obviously absorbing the information.

"Tell you what," said Mitch. "I think I can do a little better than an autograph. Davey, you drop me an email through the Tigers' website, and I'll hook us up with some tickets to the next Houston game."

Five sets of eyes went wide. "Seriously, man?"

"You bet." He draped an arm across Jenny's shoulders. "But right now I've got some pizza getting cold."

"Oh, man!"

"That's awesome!"

"Thank you, sir!"

The boys' calls of appreciation followed them as he steered Jenny along the path to the restaurant veranda.

"Were you serious about that?" she asked.

"The tickets?"

"No. Well, you better have been serious about the tickets."

"I was."

"I meant about Cole. I assume Cole was the baseball player in your story."

"He was."

She twisted her head to stare up at him. "Cole *owns* part of the Texas Tigers?"

"He owns a company that owns part of the Texas Tigers."

"Why hasn't he ever said anything?"

"To who? I knew. I expect plenty of other people did, too."

"I never knew."

He gave her shoulder a reflexive squeeze. "You're smart, Jenny. But nobody knows everything."

She harrumphed. "Well, now I know this."

"Does that put him on your husband list?"

Jenny immediately jerked away from Mitch's arm, glaring at him, putting a few feet of distance between them while her voice ramped up an octave. "How dare you?"

He wasn't really sure how he'd dared. The question had just popped out.

"Have I ever done anything to make you think I'd marry a man for his money?"

"I only just found out you wanted to get married at all." Though he supposed he'd long since suspected. Jenny was exactly the kind of girl who should settle down with a family. She'd be a great mother, an amazing wife.

He swallowed against a dry throat.

"And I am exceedingly sorry I ever told you that." She put her nose in the air and flounced toward the veranda, ending the conversation.

Five

Jenny kicked off her boots and tossed her small purse onto one of the two queen-size beds in the opulent hotel room in downtown Houston. It was nearly two in the morning. The excitement of the game and party had long since worn off, and now she was simply exhausted.

"I don't understand why you said no," Emily said as she dropped down onto the couch that faced two blue upholstered armchairs in front of a bay window offering a view of the night-time city.

"To Mitch, fixing me up? You don't see an inherent conflict there?"

"You mean because you're in love with him?"

"I am *not* in love with him," she quickly denied. "I was temporarily infatuated with him. And, sure, I slept with him. But I recognized my mistake, and I'm moving on."

"So, where's the conflict? Heck, I'd like him to set me up. Did you get a look at some of his friends?"

Jenny sat down in one of the armchairs, curling her feet

beneath her. "Like Cole? You two looked pretty cozy when we got back to the table."

Emily blew out a disgusted breath and waved her hand through the air. "Cole? Why do you think I'd handicap my children's genetics by hooking up with Cole?"

"Cole's brilliant."

"He's barely five foot ten. And this is Texas. You don't think my sons will want to try out for the football team someday?"

"Cole plays baseball."

Emily arched a brow. "This is Texas," she repeated.

"You don't even like football."

"But my kids will. And I can rah rah on the sidelines along with any good mother."

"Okay. How about this? Cole owns twenty percent of the Texas Tigers."

That information seemed to give Emily pause. "Seriously?"

"That's what Mitch just told me." Jenny's thoughts went back to their conversation. "You know, Mitch was awfully good with those teenagers. We were right in the middle of an argument, but he just switched on the charm."

"That's our Mitch. Diplomatic and charming, no matter what the circumstances."

As she digested Emily's words, an unsettling thought crept into Jenny's mind, hollowing out her stomach. "Do you think..." she began slowly. "Do you think he does it with me?"

"Does what?"

"Turns on the diplomacy. In the office. When we're together. Do you think I've been seeing the polished, professional Mitch, and not the real guy?"

"It's possible," Emily ventured. "It does seem to be second nature to him."

"And it's exactly why they appointed him to the interim presidency. He can smooth things over, make everyone feel happy, even when he's telling them no." Jenny swallowed. "Oh, dear. This is humiliating."

"Why?"

"He's been handling me, just like he handles everyone else. I had a crush on the persona. I don't even know the real guy." Jenny stood up and paced across the room. "Do you think that's why he slept with me?" When she thought back to the conversation, she felt the blood drain from her face. "The last thing I said to him before he got all gooey and romantic was that I was upset he hadn't noticed my new look. Then, all of a sudden, he couldn't say enough flowery things."

She hung her head, shoulders drooping. "He fed me a line. He told me exactly what I wanted to hear. Good grief, I've seen him do it to a hundred different people. And then, when I practically threw myself into his arms…" Jenny couldn't bring herself to finish the thought. She could never, ever face Mitch again.

"It was a mercy—" Emily pressed her lips shut.

"Just kill me," Jenny squeaked. "Toss me off the balcony, and put me out of my misery."

Emily came to her feet. "It's not that bad."

"Not that *bad*?"

Emily braced her hands on Jenny's shoulders. "He can't read your mind. All he knows is that the two of you had a one-night fling. If it was an unemotional fling for him, there's no reason it wasn't an unemotional fling for you. He wants to put it behind you. You do, too. Case closed."

"Case closed?" Jenny found her voice trembling.

"You're a logical woman, Jenny. And putting it behind you makes good sense. Heck, you've seen him a dozen times since that night. You've made it through the awkwardness. The tough part is over."

"Yes." Jenny forced herself to nod in agreement. The tough part was over. She'd do her job, professionally and thoroughly, just like she'd always done. Mitch was diplomatic. She could be just as diplomatic. And she'd keep her emotions well away from anything to do with Mitch.

"You going to let him fix you up?" asked Emily.

"Not a chance."

"You want Cole?"

"I think of Cole as a brother."

An odd expression flitted across Emily's face. "Really?"

"He's a sweetheart."

"He's stubborn as a mule. I think it's short-man syndrome."

"He's barely under six feet. And he's incredibly fit." Jenny knew that Cole was involved in martial arts. He also still played baseball, and he loved the outdoors.

"Whatever," said Emily. "He's off the list. Fortunately for us, there are still ten million other men in Texas."

And Jenny was going to be happy with one of those ten million men. She was going to find someone kind and honest, who was as interested as she was in building a loving family.

It was nearly four o'clock the following Saturday. Jenny was at the Cattleman's Club offices, finishing work on her database before the office opened up again on Monday. She'd taken over the big boardroom, spreading the membership correspondence out in a way that wasn't possible at her desk.

Her laptop was at one end of the oval table, and she had letters, emails, reports and drawings sorted in neat piles over its expanse. She was almost finished with the metadata, and she'd already scanned each of the paper documents to provide easy access for the Board of Directors.

"Jenny?" Mitch's voice echoed from outside in the hallway, footsteps coming closer. "Is that you?"

"In here," she called, trying hard not to react emotionally to his presence. She'd never had any problem with equanimity before, dealing with all kinds of people on all kinds of issues. But with Mitch logic and reason seemed to fly out the window.

"What are you doing here?" he asked through the doorway.

"I needed to finish up and get this table cleared off," she replied without looking up. She pointed from pile to pile in explanation. "Letters against a new clubhouse. Letters against a female president. Pledges to vote for a female president. Letters in support of a new clubhouse. Suggestions for elements of a new clubhouse. And, actual spec, architectural drawings of a new clubhouse. Oh, and these ones are miscellaneous, save the whales, ban antibiotics in dairy cattle, nationalize the high-tech sector and turn the stop sign at Fifth and Continental into a traffic light. I wasn't going to include them in the database."

"Somebody thinks we control the traffic lights?"

"Apparently. Can you get right on that? The letter writer believes it's a serious problem." She glanced up to see not just Mitch, but Mitch, Jeffrey and two other men that she vaguely remembered from the football team clustered in the doorway.

Her face heated. "Uh…"

Mitch strode into the room. "Jenny, these are some of my teammates. Emilio, Nathan and you already know Jeffrey."

"Of course I do. Hi, Jeffrey." She greeted the other two with a smile and a nod.

"Hey, Jenny." Jeffrey made his way around the table toward her.

The man named Emilio spoke up. He was huge, with an impossibly deep chest, jet-black hair and no discernible neck. He took in the piles on the boardroom table. "You ever want an administrative job with a football team, I'll give you a good reference."

"Back off," Mitch growled. "I'd be lost without her."

Jenny ruthlessly reminded herself that Mitch meant in a professional way. On the personal side, she was just another in a long line of dalliances.

"It's easy enough to see why," said Nathan. He was blond, and slighter than the other three, with a wide, white smile. "Great to meet you, Jenny."

"I'm giving the guys a tour of the clubhouse," Mitch explained. "But, do you want some help here?"

She quickly shook her head. "I'm almost done. The boardroom's booked by the Hospital Fundraising Auxiliary at ten tomorrow, and I wanted to make sure my mess was out of the way."

Jeffrey moved closer. "I don't mind lending a hand."

"Ten minutes, tops," Jenny assured him.

"Then I'll still be around and help you carry it all back to the office," said Jeffrey.

Mitch stepped in, an edge to his voice. "Leave everything here. We'll move it after you're done."

"But—" She caught Mitch's expression and stopped short. "Sure. Okay. Give me fifteen?"

"We'll be back," said Mitch.

Nathan spoke up. "And then you can come to dinner with us."

"Barbecue at Mitch's place," Emilio sang, clapping Mitch on the shoulder with a meaty hand.

Jenny automatically cringed, knowing it was Mitch's injured shoulder, and that he'd had a physio session scheduled for this morning. But, other than a slight tightening of his lips, Mitch didn't react.

"And bring Emily," said Jeffrey, doing a mock golf swing. "We're hitting the links first, and I need to show off to someone."

Jenny couldn't help but smile at that. She appreciated Jeffrey's happy-go-lucky approach to life. "You mean a hundred thousand screaming fans doesn't do it for you?"

"We don't have a game this week. Besides, I prefer my adoration up close and personal."

"Fifteen minutes?" Mitch confirmed, with a scowl at Jeffrey.

Jenny noticed that Mitch didn't echo the dinner invitation. Just as well. The last thing she needed was to hang out and get personal at Mitch's house. It had been a long week, with Jenny sticking carefully to professional topics only, fearing he'd bring up matchmaking again.

After the men filed out, she quickly finished the data entry, saved everything to the server and shut down her laptop. She took it back to the office, fully intending to clean up the boardroom and escape before the men made it back from the club-house tour.

Her plan failed.

She met them in the hallway on her second trip, her arms full of paper.

"I thought I told you to leave it," Mitch barked.

She immediately understood her blunder. Mitch had been trying to help her graciously exit. He'd expected her to leave the mess and clear out before they got back.

"Sorry, boss," she mumbled, feeling foolish. She could have escaped, should have escaped. This was one time when she should have ignored her instincts to finish a job before leaving work.

"It's not a problem, Mitch," Nathan put in. "I'll grab the rest, and we can head over to the golf course."

They all looked expectantly at Jenny.

"Um." She bit down on her lip, mind scrambling for an excuse. She'd never been a good liar, and trying to do it under pressure made it that much worse. "I don't think I can—" Her glance darted automatically to Mitch.

"Mitch wants you to come." Emilio clapped him on the shoulder again.

This time Mitch did cringe with obvious pain. "Of course you're welcome to come along, Jenny. Call Emily. Let's make it a party."

"Emily's hot," said Jeffrey, and Nathan and Emilio each gave a whoop of approval.

Mitch turned on them. "If you guys are going to behave like children…"

The men immediately sobered and shook their heads. "Nope. Not us. We'll be perfect gentlemen."

"Listen," Jenny put in. "It's not the most convenient day for me—"

"Call Emily," Jeffrey interrupted. "I want to impress her with my 9-iron."

Nathan and Emilio guffawed, and Mitch compressed his lips.

"I'm going to assume you didn't mean that the way it sounded," Jenny couldn't help putting in.

"Absolutely not." Jeffrey gave Nathan a shove with his shoulder. "I meant it literally."

Jenny looked to Mitch once more. His eyes were softer this time, and there was a hint of a smile on his face. "You want me to call her?" he asked.

"I can do it," Jenny capitulated.

There was every chance Emily would enjoy meeting Mitch's other teammates. They were certainly larger than Cole. Emilio, for example, could probably give her some monster, future linebacker sons.

Emily and Emilio.

It could work.

Since Mitch had his own clubs, he waited outside the pro shop while the attendant got the others outfitted.

To his surprise, Jenny joined him there. She'd avoided him as much as possible all week. And when they did end up together, both of them danced around each other, keeping the conversation strictly business. Mitch knew he should step up and make good on his offer to matchmake. It would be better for both of them if she was taken by some nice guy who'd give her that dream life. But he couldn't seem to bring himself to do it.

She came closer now, lowering her voice, suspicion written all over her face. "Please tell me this isn't a setup."

He kept his own tone low. "You think I've set you up to look bad at golf?"

Her expression shifted to a look that clearly questioned his intellect. "Not golf."

It took him a moment to realize she was talking about the matchmaking. And in that instant, he realized he could never do it. He especially couldn't set her up with his friends or team-mates. Because, if Jeffrey or one of the other guys actually did date her, fall in love with her and marry her, there was a good chance Mitch would end up lusting after a friend's wife.

If that happened, he'd have to move to Mongolia. He didn't think they played a lot of ball in Mongolia.

"It's not a setup," he assured her.

"Why don't I believe you?"

"I'm not even the one who invited you along."

"You didn't uninvite me, either."

"And you didn't come up with an excuse not to come. Even though I gave you every opportunity."

"I'm a bad liar. Sue me."

She was right about that. Jenny was smart, efficient and dedicated. But she couldn't tell a lie to save her life.

"I think Jeffrey likes you," Mitch found himself taunting.

He didn't know why he did it. Frustration, maybe. Or maybe he simply wanted to elicit an emotional reaction. Jenny was back in her uptight clothes, white blouse, pressed slacks, her glasses perched on her nose, her features carefully controlled.

He wanted more. And it worked.

Behind the glasses, her green eyes blazed defiance. "Well, I like Jeffrey."

Mitch fought his instincts. "Good."

"Darn right, it's good."

"Then he can golf with us. Hey, Jeffrey. You, me and Jenny. The rest of you can make a foursome."

Cole, who had met up with them when Mitch picked up his clubs, beamed at the groupings. There was no denying he had a thing for Emily. The woman didn't seem inclined to give him the time of day, but Cole was nothing if not tenacious. And as a baseball player in football-crazy Royal, he'd dealt with adversity his entire life.

"You're golfing with *me?*" Jenny demanded.

"How else am I going to throw you at Jeffrey?"

"But you said—"

"I guess I lied."

After a moment's silence, she stuck her prim, little nose in the air and gave a toss of her sleek hair. "Fine. Go for it. Throw us together. Let's see what happens." She sashayed back to the clubhouse.

Watching her leave, Mitch's hand tightened on his golf bag. Despite his threat, he was not going to throw Jenny and Jeffrey together, not today, not ever.

Every instinct he had told him to go after her and claim her for himself. But he had no right to do that. So instead, he hoisted his clubs and stalked toward the cart parking area.

He stuffed his clubs in the back of a cart and sat down to cool off.

When he saw the other six approach, Emilio and Jeffrey each with two golf bags on their broad shoulders, he realized he'd left Jenny to manage her own clubs. What the hell was the matter with him? Jenny was going to think he was a cad.

He sighed.

Just as well.

She might as well know the truth.

He turned on the cart ignition, while Jeffrey climbed in beside him, and Jenny sat stiffly down in the backseat.

"We're going to tee off first," said Jeffrey.

That made sense, since the three of them would complete the game faster than the other four.

They drove to the first tee.

Mitch's first swing sent his ball to the far end of the fairway, while Jeffrey's hit the green. Jenny's shot came up short, off in the rough, only a third of the way down the fairway.

"Sorry," she mumbled, shoving her 3-wood back in the bag.

"You need a few pointers?" asked Jeffrey, swinging himself into the backseat of the cart to sit next to her, leaving Mitch to be the chauffeur.

"Sure," she responded with what sounded to Mitch like enthusiasm.

"She's doing fine," Mitch intervened. "The poor woman's up against two pro football players."

"Doesn't mean she can't improve her stance and her follow-through," Jeffrey argued.

Mitch spent the next six holes watching Jeffrey play the attentive instructor to Jenny the naive golf student. He had her listening with rapt attention, concentrating, improving her swing, laughing at her own mistakes, while Mitch's mood darkened along with the clouds rolling in from the Gulf.

On the seventh fairway, the first raindrops splattered down.

"Let's finish this one and head back," Mitch called down the fairway to Jeffrey, relieved that the torturous afternoon was about to end.

He waited while Jenny lined up a shot on the far side of the fairway.

Suddenly, thunder split the sky above them, lightning tracing its way across the arc of the black clouds.

"Don't swing!" he yelled to Jenny, abandoning his ball to sprint toward her.

She twisted her head to stare at him in confusion.

He pointed to the sky. "There's lightning up there. Your club's a conductor."

As he reached her and snagged the club from her hands, the skies opened up above them.

Mitch quickly glanced around for shelter. "The gazebo," he called, grabbing her hand to make a run for it. The golf cart was farther away, where Jeffrey had left it on the path.

Jeffrey saw their move, and dashed in the same direction.

By the time the three of them made it to the small open-sided cedar gazebo, it was pouring rain, and they were soaked to the skin.

"Crap," Jeffrey sputtered, running his hand over his wet hair and shaking out the droplets.

Jenny was in a short-sleeved white blouse, topping a pair

of pale gray slacks. The blouse clung to her torso, outlining a lacy bra.

Jeffrey's brows went up as he took in an eyeful, but Mitch stepped between them, warning Jeffrey off with a glare.

Mitch quickly stripped off his navy golf shirt and handed it to Jenny.

She looked perplexed. "What are you—"

"You're translucent," he explained.

She glanced down. "Oh."

"Put it on, Jenny."

She snagged the shirt from his hand and tugged it over her head, settling the hem around her thighs, then finger combing her damp hair.

"I didn't expect to go swimming," she huffed.

Jeffrey grinned, peeping over Mitch's shoulder. "No complaints from me."

"Back off," Mitch warned.

"It's a forty-dollar bra." Jenny brushed off the incident. "Models wear them on the runway all the time, in nationally televised shows no less."

"You want to give me my shirt back?" he challenged.

"Not really." Then her gaze froze for a moment on his bare chest.

He dared to hope she liked what she saw. Then he gave himself an instant rebuke. How would that be good? This physical attraction between him and Jenny was the root cause of all their problems.

The lightning flashed, the thunder boomed and the rain came down even harder.

"You want me to go get the cart?" Jeffrey offered.

"We might as well wait it out a few minutes," said Mitch. "This might not last long."

Jenny's cell phone rang.

She pulled up the tail of Mitch's shirt and dug into the pocket of her slacks. "It's probably Emily. I hope they're all okay. Hello?" she said into the phone.

She listened for a moment, eyes narrowing, mouth turning into a frown.

"Everything all right?" Mitch couldn't help but ask, but she waved him to silence and turned her back.

He glanced to Jeffrey, whose brow furrowed in concern. Had somebody been hurt?

"Uh-huh," Jenny was saying, her tone grave. "No. No, I don't." Her free hand went to her forehead, and Mitch reflexively stepped toward her.

"Jenny?" He put a hand on her shoulder.

"As soon as I can," she said without acknowledging him. "Yes. Of course." She blew out a breath.

"Jenny?" Mitch repeated.

She turned to him, her face pale, hands shaking as she lowered the phone. "My house is on fire."

"*What?* What happened? Who was on the phone?"

"My neighbor. It was a lightning strike." Jenny held up helpless palms. "The roof burst into flames."

Mitch grabbed her phone before it could slide off to the floor. "Has the fire department been notified?"

"They're on the way there."

"I'll get the cart," said Jeffrey, bounding down the two stairs to sprint across the course.

Mitch reached out to touch Jenny's arm, longing to pull her into his embrace. "No pets, right?"

"That's what Clara, my neighbor, asked. No. No pets. I'm allergic to cats."

Mitch hadn't known that. He tried to rub the chill from her shoulders. "It might not be so bad. The rain will help put the fire out. And the fire department's close by."

Jenny nodded numbly. Then she seemed to gather herself. "You're right. No sense borrowing trouble." She gave a decisive

nod. "We need the facts. Let's get the facts, and go from there."
She stepped away from his hand.

Mitch's protective instincts nearly blinded him. Jenny be-
longed in the comfort of his arms, not standing there all alone
and dripping wet, trying to cope with the disaster that had
suddenly befallen her life.

He made a move toward her, giving in, anticipating the feel
of her small body against his.

But Jeffrey was pulling up in the cart. And Jenny was darting
for the gazebo stairs. And the moment was gone.

Six

Red-and-blue lights flashed against the chaos that was once Jenny's home. A dozen firemen sprayed water into her windows, where orange flames leaped out in the darkening evening. Neighbors stood on the sidewalks, huddled under umbrellas, avoiding the runoff that had turned to a gushing river cascading down the street. The rain remained steady, but Jenny barely noticed.

Emily linked an arm with hers, squeezing tight. "Thank goodness you weren't home."

Jenny swallowed. She hadn't thought of that. But it was true. If the guys hadn't invited her to go golfing, she might have been sitting in her living room, directly below the lightning strike.

She shuddered reflexively at the thought.

"It's going to be okay," Emily continued.

Jenny nodded, trying to force her rational mind to engage. There was a lot to be thankful for here.

"I know," she finally said. "Nobody was hurt. And everything else is just stuff. It can all be replaced." She paused, a dark shot of humor piercing her numbness. "It's not like I had boxes of precious mementos from my happy childhood."

"Okay, that was impressive," said Emily.

"What?"

"You. Looking on the bright side so quickly."

Jenny shrugged. "I suppose I could curl up in a fetal position somewhere and cry instead."

"Many people would."

"I think I'm in shock."

"Yes, well, that's to be expected. You've got insurance, right?"

Jenny nodded. She was well insured. Everything being destroyed by the fire could be replaced.

Her brain automatically began to catalog the possessions in her house. She started in the living room, where the fire was worst, then she mentally worked her way through the dining room, kitchen and bedroom.

"We are going to have to replace my new wardrobe," she pointed out to Emily.

"That part'll be fun," Emily responded with determined cheerfulness.

Jenny didn't disagree. Shopping for new clothes with Emily had been a lot of fun. Of course, shopping for every single possession a person needed in life was a little more daunting.

She told herself she was lucky. The circumstances of her childhood made very little of her life irreplaceable.

"At least there are no homemade quilts. No heirloom jewelry," she reminded Emily.

"That's a good thing," said Emily. Then she gestured to the fire. "At a time like this."

Emily knew all about Jenny's complicated upbringing. Her parents had gotten married because her mother was pregnant with Jenny. The marriage was a mistake, and after five rocky years, her father had left them for good. After the breakup, her mother's psychological and emotional issues had grown worse, making life chaotic for young Jenny.

Just then, a section of the carport caved in, landing with a resounding crash on top of her car. She started at the sound, blowing out a breath.

"Gonna need a new car, too." Emily's voice was hoarse.

"This is unbelievable." Jenny struggled to keep her equilibrium. Her possessions were disintegrating in front of her eyes.

She caught a glimpse of Mitch where he stood next to the fire truck. He seemed to sense something, turning to scan the crowd. When he came to Jenny and Emily, the scan stopped. He looked directly into her eyes for a moment before returning to his conversation with the fire chief. Meanwhile Cole and the teammates looked on, obviously ready for action, and just as obviously frustrated by their inability to pitch in.

"Do you think this is a sign?" Emily asked.

Jenny dragged her gaze away from Mitch. "A sign of what?"

"That it's time to start a new life?"

"You mean leave town?" Leave Royal, the TCC, Mitch?

"No. No. I was thinking that when you rebuild, you could go sleek and modern, instead of boxy and practical."

"You didn't like my house?" Jenny was surprised to hear that. It was... Her gaze fixed on the flames once more. Well, at least it had once been very functional and livable. It had everything Jenny needed, and the mortgage was very nearly paid off.

"I'm just saying, maybe something that goes along with the new clothes, the new hairstyle, the new makeup and, soon, the new man."

Jenny pondered the suggestion.

A fresh start. Wasn't that exactly what she'd been telling herself she needed? Was the universe trying to help her out?

"The TCC is awash with both professional and amateur architects," she noted. "The building project is bringing everyone with a drafting table out of the woodwork."

"Anyone have a style you particularly like?"

"A couple, for sure." Jenny nodded. There were some incredibly creative people living in Royal.

"There you go. Think about it. Maybe do something completely different, fun, exciting."

"You suppose there's something wrong with us?" Jenny took a step back as the flames grew hotter on her face.

"Not a thing," said Emily.

"We're standing here planning my new house while the old one burns."

"It means we're practical," Emily stated with conviction. "Practical and realistic. Those are both very admirable traits."

Jenny watched while a fireman doused the oak tree overhanging her living room roof. The roof was blackened, and sagging at an unnatural angle. She couldn't help picturing the armchair that sat in front of the bay window. She'd bought it last year on sale over in Westbury County. There was a tear on the back now, and she'd never been really crazy about the plaid pattern.

Truth be told, she'd also been thinking about replacing her television set. Though, in this day and age, maybe a larger computer monitor made more sense.

"You must be getting cold." Mitch's voice startled her, and she realized he'd moved up next to her in the darkening night. The lights seemed to flash brighter now, the flames more vivid, though she knew the fire was coming under control.

"I'm hot," she responded, wiping her damp hands across her fire-warmed cheeks.

"The fire will be out soon. And you're still soaking wet."

"So is everybody else." She couldn't help stealing a glance at Mitch's bare, glistening chest. She was still wearing his T-shirt, and he looked magnificent, somehow all-powerful standing amidst the chaos.

"I talked to the chief," he continued. "They think the lightning fried your entire electrical system and started a bunch of smaller fires inside the walls. There's really nothing more you can do here tonight." His gaze shifted to Emily. "Is Jenny going to stay with you?"

"Not unless she wants to swell up like a blowfish."

Mitch's brows went up in an unspoken question.

"My cats," said Emily.

Jenny's nose twitched and her sinuses tingled just thinking about Powder and Puff, Emily's long-haired Persians. She was good for a couple of hours at Emily's. But she'd never be able to sleep overnight. "I guess it'll have to be a hotel."

The Family Inn by the highway had kitchenettes, and their rates were reasonable. She struggled not to feel overwhelmed by the logistics of the next few days. There'd be necessities to purchase, insurance forms to fill out, and soon, very soon, she was sure the magnitude of her loss would hit her.

"Why don't we all head for my place for now," Mitch suggested, his broad hand coming down on Jenny's shoulder. The gesture felt far too comforting, so she quickly shrugged it off. She couldn't let herself depend on Mitch.

"We'll get everybody dried off," he continued, clearing his throat and letting his hand drop to his side. "We can have something to eat and figure out your next steps."

"Good idea," Emily quickly agreed.

Jenny followed up on Emily's agreement with a nod. The chill of the night air was setting in as the bright flames turned to billowing smoke, and the mist from the fire hoses mixed with the steady rain coming down on them.

Jenny couldn't stay here and stare much longer. She had to get started on the logistics of the rest of her life.

Since Jenny's entire wardrobe had gone up in smoke, Mitch had asked Cole to stop at the Quick-Mart and pick her up a pair of sweatpants and a warm shirt that would fit. He'd offered her his shower, then put a barbecued cheeseburger directly into her hands, making sure she had a comfortable place to sit and an opportunity to collect her thoughts.

Now, with the barbecue finished and cleaned up, and a friendly poker game underway in his dining room, he watched

Jenny wander out onto his deck alone. She stopped at the rail to gaze across the lights of the golf course. The rain had stopped about an hour ago, and the moon was peeking out from behind the dissipating storm clouds.

Mitch waved off an invitation to join in the game and followed her outside.

Her feet were bare on the damp deck, since Cole hadn't thought to buy socks or shoes, and hers were still in a heap in Mitch's laundry room. Mitch briefly glanced to where the fleece pants covered her rear end and wondered if Cole had thought to buy underwear. But he quickly squelched that picture, admonishing his wandering imagination.

If there was a scrap of a gentleman inside him, she needed it right now. He made himself promise to provide her with support, not lust.

"Hey," he offered softly, padding across the cool, smooth deck, his own feet also bare after he'd changed from wet clothes to a pair of faded jeans and a well-worn Tigers T-shirt.

She turned her head to profile, mustering up a weak smile. The hoots and good-natured ribbing of the poker game faded behind him.

"You okay?" His voice was gentle as he came to a halt next to her at the rail.

She shrugged her slim shoulders, turning her attention back to the view. For some reason, she looked particularly delicate beneath the oversized navy hooded shirt. "I'm fine."

He didn't believe that for a minute. "Yeah, right."

"I'm really fine."

"You've just lost everything you own." Mitch couldn't imagine every treasure and memento of his entire life, his childhood trophies, the faded football jerseys, certificates, photographs, letters, gifts from his parents' travels around the world, going up in flames before his eyes.

She turned to look at him, tone going a bit brittle. "Thank you so much for pointing that out."

"Jenny."

"No, really. I'd almost forgotten."

He set his jaw. He could take this. She deserved to be upset. And if she needed to rail, it might as well be at him.

But she fell silent.

"Go ahead," he invited.

"What?"

"Get it out. Yell at me."

Her tone had returned to normal. "How would that help?"

Now, he was the one feeling frustrated. "Quit being so damn logical and analytical. You do what you have to do."

She glanced down at the baggy clothes. "What I have to do is go shopping. I may be a little late for work tomorrow, boss."

"You know that's not what I meant."

"What did you mean?"

"I meant emotionally. You deserve to be angry, to rail at the universe. Let it out, Jenny."

Nobody, not even logical, practical, two-feet-firmly-planted-on-the-ground Jenny could go through a disaster like this and not feel distraught.

"There's nothing to let out," she told him.

"Yes, there is."

But instead of answering, she got a faraway look in her green eyes. Moments ticked by. But, finally, she spoke. "I know you must find it odd."

Since he hadn't a clue what she was talking about, he waited for her to elaborate.

"Emily said I should rebuild." Jenny leaned back, holding herself steady with a firm grip around the top rail. "That sounded good to me. I rather like the idea of starting from scratch, building a life that reflects who I am today, and not..." Her voice trailed away.

He waited.

"What must I find odd?" he finally asked.

"I hear what you're saying." She seemed to wander off on yet another conversational tangent. "A normal person would be a little upset that everything she owned had just turned to ashes."

"A little upset?"

Jenny did have a gift for understatement.

"Thing is," she continued. "I don't really care."

"Of course you care." Clearly, the woman was in shock. Or maybe she was in denial. Was there something he ought to do about either of those conditions? Or did they simply work themselves out over time?

She shook her head. "I don't care. It's stuff, Mitch. I can get new stuff."

"It's not the stuff itself," he felt compelled to point out. "It's stuff as the representation of your life, your achievements, your milestones."

"I guess I have no achievements."

"That's ridiculous."

Jenny was one of the most accomplished people he knew. The TCC couldn't run without her. Mitch wouldn't even want to try.

She gave a little shiver. "Maybe this isn't the best time—" Then she laughed. "Or maybe you're not the best person."

He reflexively reached for the propane heater switch, flicking it on, causing three tall, strategically placed heaters to glow to life. He sure didn't like thinking that he wasn't the best person to help Jenny.

"We should drop it," she told him.

"You have dozens, maybe hundreds of accomplishments," he told her. "Ask ten other people in Royal, and they'll tell you exactly the same thing."

"You're not dropping it," she pointed out.

"Because you're not making sense."

"My house just burned down. I'm allowed to not make sense."

"Are you in shock?" He scanned her face. She wasn't pale, and she wasn't shaking. In fact, all things considered, she looked remarkably calm.

"Just because I don't have a stash of silly little life mementos that are vulnerable to loss or destruction, doesn't mean I'm in shock."

Mitch tried to figure out what she meant. "Everybody has mementos." Whatever they were, she had to be upset at losing them.

She gave a cold laugh. "Hard for the all-American kid to understand, huh? We didn't all live that storybook childhood, Mitch."

Mitch hadn't lived a perfect childhood. Far from it. "Are you angry with me?"

"No. I'm not angry with anyone." She backed away from the rail and plunked down on one of the couches. "Let's talk about you instead."

Mitch hesitated. But he knew people reacted to stress in different ways, and he should probably humor her. He took the chair across from her. "What do you want to know?"

"Tell me about your mementos. What would it absolutely kill you to lose in a fire?"

Besides Jenny?

Not a good answer.

He gave it some thought. "My Fitzpatrick Trophy."

"Why?"

"Because they're hard to win. And it's the rookie of the year award. It's not like I'm ever going to be a rookie again."

"So, it reminds you of something good?"

"Yeah." Well, sort of. It mostly reminded him of his hard-ass dad, and how Mitch had finally stuck it to the old man by proving that he wasn't a complete screwup. Still, who wouldn't hate to lose the Fitzpatrick in a fire?

"Winning it was immensely satisfying," he said to Jenny.

She gazed at him for a long moment. "What else?"

"I don't know. The usual stuff. Pictures, certificates, ribbons, my college diploma. Why are we talking about me?"

"Because it's more fun than talking about me."

"No, it's not." Mitch would rather talk about Jenny any day of the week. In fact, now that the subject had come up, he found himself with a burning curiosity. "What, exactly, did you lose tonight?"

"Well, it sure wasn't any rookie of the year trophy," she finally offered.

"Other things are just as important as sports trophies. Pictures of your tenth birthday party, for instance. Or that stellar report card I just know you got in first grade and every other grade after that." He'd be willing to bet that even back then, Jenny had been pretty much perfect, always punctual, always neat, all work complete and in on time. In short, a teacher's dream.

He smiled encouragingly, but Jenny's eyes had clouded to jade. Had he just reminded her that she'd lost all her childhood photographs?

What a complete cad.

Impulsively, he moved to the couch beside her.

"No tenth birthday pictures," she said.

Not anymore. Mitch could have kicked himself.

"No report cards." Using both hands, she raked her fingers through her damp hair. "Funny thing about my mother." She leaned back and tipped her head against the couch.

Mitch wanted to reach out to her, but he forced himself to stay still. Something important was obviously going on inside her head.

"She liked to clean," said Jenny.

Okay, that wasn't what he'd expected. "Clean?" he prompted.

"A lot." Jenny stifled a small laugh with the back of her hand. "You've heard of hoarders?"

"Of course."

"Mom was the opposite. It was some kind of an obsessive-compulsive disorder. She's on medication now. But, well, let's just say I'm pretty accustomed to starting over when it comes to worldly possessions."

Mitch found himself moving closer. "What are you saying?"

"I'm saying she got rid of things. Every year or so, in a fit of psychological confusion, she would throw out every single thing in my bedroom."

Mitch was struck silent.

"I tried so hard when I was little," Jenny continued, a faraway look coming into her eyes. "I thought if I kept everything in my room just so." She gestured with both hands. "Neat as a pin, dolls lined up by size, their clothes ironed, pictures alphabetical, socks in the top drawer, underwear next, pajamas, tops and skirts and slacks." Her voice faded away.

"You ironed your doll clothes?" He couldn't keep the incredulity out of his tone.

"It didn't help. She cleaned them all out anyway."

Mitch felt as though he'd been given an astonishing window into Jenny's makeup. "Is that why you're so meticulous and efficient?"

"In small doses, it's a good thing."

"But do you like being meticulous and efficient?" It had never once occurred to him that she might not. Did she get satisfaction out of running a tight ship at the office, or was it a leftover compulsion from her childhood?

Laughter wafted out from the raucous poker game, as Emily accused Cole of being a jinx.

Jenny didn't answer, and Mitch realized he didn't know her nearly as well as he thought he had. Was she unhappy? Did she struggle emotionally?

"You can change, you know," he told her.

"I have changed."

"I don't mean putting on a sexy dress for a wedding and getting all gorgeous—"

She laid her index finger across his lips, but it was too late. The image was already coursing through his brain. And the touch of her finger put a physical element into the fantasy.

He was going to kiss her again.

Unless lightning struck him dead, he was going to lean in, capture her lips and drag her into his arms all over again.

From the poker table, Cole gloated in triumph, reminding Mitch that they were in full view of five other people. But he didn't even care.

He captured her hand, holding it tight against his cheek. When he spoke, his voice was strangled. "What am I going to do about you, Jenny?"

A beat went past.

"Take me to a hotel."

For a split second, he misunderstood and desire roared to life. But then he got it. "You meant without me."

Her cheeks flushed bright, and her lips flattened together, her entire body stiffening with anger. "It's not fair for you to send me mixed signals like that. What is it you want, Mitch?"

"What I want, and what I can have are two completely different things." He knew he was wrong. He was doubly wrong to say it out loud, and it was unforgivable to say it to Jenny. But that didn't change the way he felt.

"You were the one who called a halt to everything," she reminded him.

The heated air suddenly felt stifling. "I explained to you why I had to do that."

"You never did."

He cataloged their conversations through his brain. Of course he'd explained it to her. What exactly had he said to her? "It's because you are you, and I am me."

She came to her feet, expression closed off. "Nice. You're the big celebrity, and I'm a boring small-town girl."

"No, you don't—"

"I understand perfectly, Mitch." Her eyes blazed, and she held up her hands. "Do me a favor. Let's keep it strictly professional from here on in. I don't want to know about your childhood, and I don't want you to know about mine."

"I threw smelly socks in the corner."

She blinked in incomprehension.

"When I was a kid," he elaborated, for some reason, refusing to let the conversation end. He wanted to know about her, and he wanted her to know about him. "And as a teenager. I used to drop my socks, my jerseys, shorts, pretty much anything, wherever they fell, and let 'em sit."

"Why are you—"

"It ticked my mother off something fierce. And my dad yelled at me for doing it. Then again, he yelled at me for every little mistake. Especially on the football field."

"Mitch—"

He ignored her interruption. "From the time I was nine years old. It didn't matter if a receiver was out of place, or if a blocker screwed up. Everything that happened on that football field was my fault. The pass wasn't long enough. It wasn't accurate enough. I should have run. I should have faked. I should have found a hole, handed off or cut back."

Mitch couldn't believe the words were tumbling out of him. He'd never shared this with anyone. "When I wasn't a first-round draft pick, he called me an abject failure. He said I hadn't put my heart into it."

Jenny was looking at him with pity now. He hated pity. But from her, he'd take it. It was better than indifference.

"But your interviews," she put into the silence. "The two of you go on camera together. And you rave about his inspiration and support."

Mitch gave a cold laugh. "I do, don't I?"

"It's all an act?"

"We have an unspoken agreement to revise history."

Jenny sat back down. "Are you trying to make me care about you?"

"Yes. No." What the hell was he trying to do here?

He took her hand, and mustered every scrap of honor in his disreputable soul. "I'm a cad and a womanizer, and I can smooth talk my way into or out of just about anything. Like touchdown passes, most things in life come way too easily to me, and I don't appreciate them nearly as much as I should."

Her eyes had softened, and he felt the danger of her compassion right down to his toes.

"Is that what your dad told you?" she asked.

"He was right."

"What if he wasn't?"

Mitch shook his head. "Don't do it, Jenny. Don't convince yourself that I'm worthy."

"Don't convince yourself that you're not."

"I'm—"

"You are a glib smooth talker, Mitch. You're smart and you're diplomatic, and I know you've been handling me just like you handle everyone else in your life. But there's more to you than that. You just proved it."

"Hate me, Jenny."

"I can't."

"If you could see inside my head right now, you'd have no trouble at all."

"Tell me what's inside your head."

No way, no how was he going to do that.

But her gaze was steady, and the heated air thickened between them.

"You are," he finally said, determined to put an end to this once and for all. It was true that he could talk his way out of anything, and right now he was going to talk his way out of Jenny. "And you're naked. On top of me. Your hair is wild, and your breasts are gleaming in the moonlight."

Her eyes went round, and her lips parted.

"You've kissed every inch of my body, and I've kissed every inch of yours. You're crying out my name, begging for more, harder, deeper. Your nails dig into my shoulder, but it feels good, because it's you. And we come together, and it lasts forever, and it's the best freaking sex I've ever had."

She gave a long, slow blink, her cheeks flushed red, and her shoulders drooping in the still, heated air.

"But guess what, Jenny?" he spat. "It's a one-night stand. The next day I go back on the road, back to the team, back to the parties and the girls, and I leave you far behind."

He let his words drop to cold silence.

Her eyes narrowed, and her lips pressed together. "You're lying."

He gave a harsh chuckle. "That's the bald-faced truth, darlin'. I'd be lying if I told you anything else."

She straightened and drew away from him.

He hated the suspicion in her eyes, but he knew it was for the best. "You're right to suspect that I'm handling you, Jenny. I can talk my way into your pants then out of your life without breaking a sweat. When it comes to sex, don't trust me for an instant."

She rose shakily to her feet, and took a couple of backward steps, staring at him in obvious shock.

It was only then that he realized Emily, Cole and Jeffrey had overheard the tail end of his little speech.

Emily quickly swooped in and put an arm around Jenny, ushering her swiftly toward the front door.

Cole gave Mitch a glare of disgust and followed the two women.

Jeffrey ambled onto the deck and took a seat as the front door slammed firmly behind the trio.

"Harsh," Jeffrey observed.

"Necessary," Mitch responded, feeling lower than turf grass.

"I've sure never seen you do that before."

"She deserves to know the truth."

"That wasn't the truth. That was you protecting someone you care about," said Jeffrey. "You were trying to scare her off."

Seven

Jenny was still stunned from Mitch's words as she blindly followed Emily and Cole into Cole's front foyer. The terra-cotta tiles were smooth and cool under her bare feet. Clearly, there was something wrong with her. Otherwise, she would simply walk away from Mitch and be done with it.

"What is the *matter* with you people?" Emily demanded of Cole as he secured the door behind them.

"Don't lump me in with him." Cole strode through a plaster archway and into the living room of his large, airy house. He swept an arm toward a curving staircase, looking at Jenny. "There are three bedrooms up there. Take whichever one you want. But you're not going anywhere near a hotel tonight or any other night."

Jenny was nearly overcome with gratitude. She just wanted everything to stop for tonight. She was tired, battered and bruised.

"He was a colossal jerk," Emily stated, stomping her way behind Cole as he moved farther into the house.

"You won't get an argument from me," Cole tossed over his shoulder.

"Maybe I should quit my job?" Jenny ventured, bringing up the rear, struggling to keep her feelings in some semblance of order. Mitch had hurt her, there was no doubt about that. But he'd also outlined the bald truth in no uncertain terms. There was absolutely no future for the two of them.

"No," was Emily's quick response.

"You'll outlast him," said Cole. "Wine, anyone? Whiskey? Beer?"

The more Jenny thought about it, the more handing in her resignation made sense. Mitch had made it as plain as possible that he wasn't interested in a relationship. But despite her vows to both herself and Emily, she couldn't seem to get him out of her head. Seeing him every day would only make things worse.

"I don't think I can face him," she told Emily.

"It's *him* that shouldn't be able to face *you*," Emily put in with staunch loyalty.

Maybe that was fair, but it wasn't reality. "Do you suppose he'd give me a reference?"

Cole chose a crystal bottle filled with amber liquid from the bar situated between the two walls of glass that showed off his backyard. "I'd give you a reference. Hell, I'll give you a job. You just say the word, Jenny. Tell me what kind of career you want, and I'll make it happen."

Jenny couldn't help but smile at Cole's generous offer. She felt immeasurably better being around such loyal friends. "You know any nice guys, Cole? Are there any nice guys left in the world?"

"I'm a nice guy." Cole splashed some whiskey into a heavy crystal tumbler.

"Would you date me?"

"You bet." But his glance flicked to Emily.

Jenny smiled at the telltale action. "Or maybe you have a

nice friend?" she amended her request. "The four of us could double."

"Excuse me?" Emily put in.

Jenny ignored her. "Anybody but Mitch."

Cole grunted at that. "You want me to fix you up?"

"I want you to fix me up."

"Don't count me in on this plan," said Emily.

Cole placed the tumbler in her hand, his fingers lingering against hers for a moment. "Nobody asked for your opinion."

"You're getting it anyway."

His gaze bore into hers. "You pick the time, the date and the location. We'll do anything you want."

Emily glared back. "It's not the location that's the problem."

"Then what's the problem?"

"You're the problem," Emily stated bluntly.

"You barely know me," Cole countered.

"You're short."

"I'm taller than you."

"Ha."

"I'm five-eleven. What are you? Five-six? Five-seven?"

"Five-six," Emily admitted.

"There you go. As long as you keep your heels below five inches, we're good. Now, where do you want to go?"

"Nowhere."

Jenny watched the battle of wills with fascination, wondering who'd come out on top. Emily was self-assured and very determined, but Cole seemed to be holding his own against her.

He cocked his head toward Jenny. "You'd abandon your best friend in her time of need?"

"Jenny has nothing to do with this."

"I'm fixing her up, helping mend her broken heart."

"My heart's not broken," Jenny felt compelled to add. Bruised, maybe. And definitely the worse for wear. But she wasn't about to let some silly schoolgirl crush incapacitate her.

"Her heart's not broken," Emily repeated, staring pointedly into Cole's eyes.

"She asked me to fix her up."

"*Her*, not *me*."

"She needs moral support. Now, where do you want to go?"

Emily pressed her lips mulishly together and, despite everything that had happened over this hellish day, Jenny fought an urge to laugh.

"I have tickets to the Longhorn Banquet in Austin next weekend," Cole offered with a sly smile.

Jenny silently awarded him a point for that one. The Longhorn Banquet was the hottest ticket of the year. Held in the state capital, it included the who's who, and celebrated prominent Texas citizens' annual accomplishments. The governor would attend, as would business, arts and sports notables from around the state.

"Wait 'til you see my jet," Cole added. "And I've rented a house on Lake Austin. Waterfront, six bedrooms, spa, pool and a full staff. Jenny can stay with us. And, I'll get her a date."

"I'm in," said Jenny. In her books, anticipating a luxurious weekend away was definitely better than wallowing in self-pity for the next week.

Emily turned to her. "You're not buying this," she exclaimed. "He's bribing us with staff, and a spa, and a private jet." Then her words trailed away.

"If I'm going to get bribed," Jenny put in philosophically. "It might as well be by the best."

Emily stared at Jenny for a long moment. Then her hand went to Cole's chest. "She's smiling. You made her smile."

"I did." Cole accepted the credit, leaning ever so imperceptibly toward Emily.

Then while Emily crossed the big room to Jenny, Cole's hungry gaze stayed glued to her every move.

"You really want to do this?" Emily asked her. "You think it'll make you feel better?"

"I sure don't want to sit on my butt and pine away for Mitch."

"He's a jerk."

"He truly is." But even as she voiced her agreement, Jenny couldn't help remembering the expression on his face when he'd told her about his father. She'd never have imagined all-American Mitch Hayward was hiding a crappy childhood. They had that in common.

"Okay." Emily nodded.

"So, it's a go?" Cole asked hopefully.

Emily shot him a warning glare. "This weekend is all about Jenny, not about you."

"Yes, ma'am." Cole grinned. "You ladies just tell me what you'd like. Meal suggestions for the chef, preferences for floral arrangements, wines, special sheets on the beds? They have chauffeur-driven SUVs, but I can get a stretch limo if you'd prefer."

Jenny nudged her friend. "How are you not dating this guy already?"

"He's too short," said Emily.

"I'll buy lifts," Cole put in.

"Short is a state of mind."

"It's a state in *your* mind, woman, not mine."

Emily sniffed her disapproval, and Jenny couldn't help but laugh.

"I'm leaving now," said Emily, and disappointment flickered in Cole's blue eyes.

Emily missed it because her attention was focused on Jenny. "I'm going to grab you some of my clothes and a few personal things. Tomorrow, we'll stock you up. But I'll be back in an hour with the essentials."

Since there was nothing left to salvage from her house, the insurance forms were straightforward, and the cleanup started right away. Jenny drove by it once, on Sunday morning, but she quickly decided it was time to focus on the future, not to dwell on the past.

The house was gone for good. But the lake was still beautiful, and the black scars on the land would heal. Emily was right. There was a lot to be said for rebuilding something brand-new, right here.

Jenny took Monday off work to dash through a long list of errands and settle into Cole's guest room. She'd offered once more to get a room at the Family Inn. But Cole was adamant, and Emily backed him up. He had plenty of room, and it would take months for her new house to be built.

It was a shock for her to find out that Cole had a housekeeping staff. He had a cook, a gardener and a housekeeper. All were incredibly friendly and seemed determined to treat Jenny like royalty. When she'd mentioned that she usually took baking to the office on Tuesdays for the TCC's youth outreach program, Maria, the cook, had insisted on pitching in to make cupcakes.

So, the mound of jumbo gourmet-frosted chocolate creations that Jenny carried outside to the athletic field late Tuesday afternoon attracted more than the usual hungry glances from the thirty or so teenage boys practicing football passes.

Mitch had started the youth outreach during his first month at TCC. He was a strong advocate for youth in sports, and his star power had ensured participation from the local teenage boys. The program had grown, and now several members of the TCC were working with the teenagers on everything from algebra to career planning. But Tuesday after school was still devoted to sports, and Jenny had taken up the habit of providing a baked treat for the kids at the end of the session.

Normally, she left the baking next to their water jug, gave everyone a wave and went back to work. But today, she found herself pausing. As angry as she wished she could be with Mitch, she couldn't help noting how great he was with the kids. And she couldn't help remembering the story about his father.

Were the two related in some way? Was he trying to do for

other kids what his own father never did for him? She recalled the encounter on the beach in Galveston. Mitch had stuck up for the smaller kid. In a few short moments, he'd obviously boosted the boy's self-esteem, and very likely given him a whole new perspective on life and on his future opportunities.

Jenny watched while Mitch gave a few pointers on passing the football to one of the boys. Again, it was one of the smaller boys, someone who might easily get picked on in a group. The boy nodded, gave another throw and was rewarded by Mitch's clap on the shoulder and what were obviously words of praise.

How on earth could Mitch think of himself as a bad guy?

Then his gaze caught Jenny's.

Since she'd skipped work yesterday, and since today he'd had back-to-back meetings out of the office, they'd barely spoken. On the upside, there'd been no time for awkward conversation. On the downside, she knew that conversation was looming in their future.

She'd written and discarded three letters of resignation yesterday. Part of her longed to walk away from the emotional minefield of working for Mitch, but the other part of her loved her job at TCC and told herself she was adult enough to stick this out.

Cole was right. One way or another, Mitch would be gone from Royal very soon, and he'd be completely out of her life. At the latest, he'd leave after the TCC presidential election in December. That wasn't so far away. Jenny could keep her head down and her focus on business until then. Heaven knew the issues surrounding the new clubhouse and the presidency were coming at them faster and more furious by the day. Who'd have time to talk about anything personal before the election?

Now Mitch was moving toward her.

The TCC building and emotional safety were just fifty yards away. She could make it if she left right now. She doubted very much that he'd sprint after her. Then, while he finished up with the boys, she could shut down her computer, gather her purse, head for the parking lot and drive her rental car back to Cole's house and hide in the back sunroom, where Mitch's house wasn't even visible.

He was closer now.

She had one minute to make a decision.

Leaving would be easy.

Staying would be fraught with—

"Hello, Jenny." His long strides quickly covered the last few yards between them.

"Hello, Mitch," she offered evenly.

His glance went to the big tray of chocolate cupcakes sitting on the table. "The boys'll like those."

"Maria made them."

He nodded. "So you did decide to stay at Cole's?"

"He didn't tell you?" That surprised Jenny. Cole and Mitch were very close friends.

"I don't believe he's speaking to me at the moment."

She didn't know how to respond to that. Emily and Cole hadn't overheard Mitch's entire kiss-off speech, thank goodness, but they'd heard enough to be very angry with Mitch. Still, she couldn't help hoping the incident wouldn't drive a wedge between the two men.

"I'm, uh, sorry," she tried.

"*You're* sorry?"

"That Cole's angry with you."

"He'll get over it." Mitch paused. "And you?"

"Me?" Was he asking if she'd get over being angry with him for not wanting a relationship with her? It sounded quite petty when she thought about it that way. It was entirely Mitch's business who he chose to date or not to date. If he wasn't interested, he wasn't interested. That surely wasn't his fault.

Still, she couldn't seem to find a coherent answer to his question, and the silence stretched between them.

He was the one to break it. "Are you going to quit, Jenny?"

She drew a breath. Mostly, she thought no. But in the dark

of night, when Mitch's words ran around and around inside her head, she sometimes felt like she had to make a clean break, if only to save her sanity.

"Let me be the one to quit," he put in before she could answer.

"What? No." She shook her head firmly in denial. "You can't quit." She gestured to the field. "The boys, the members, everyone depends on you. I'm completely expendable."

He took a step closer. "You've got it backward. I'm a figurehead. You're the one who's indispensable."

It wasn't true, but the earnestness in his eyes suddenly brought home the humor of the conversation. "Is it just me," she asked him, "or is our mutual admiration society a little nauseating?"

Mitch broke into a familiar grin, and a wave of relief coursed through Jenny's stomach. He stage whispered, "I'll keep it a secret if you do."

"Definitely."

His expression sobered again. "And I'll stay if you will."

Jenny gathered her courage. "Okay. I'll stay." She risked another joke. "But you have to promise to keep your hands to yourself."

"You're a pistol, Jenny."

"I'm a survivor, Mitch."

A funny expression crossed his face. "You don't have to *survive* the TCC, Jenny. You're fantastic at your job. Don't worry so much about being careful and meticulous. Relax a little. You can make mistakes and mess things up. Nobody will die."

She understood what he was saying. She didn't have to be perfect for him. For some reason, his words made her eyes sting.

She blinked quickly to get rid of the sensation. "Does that sound like me? Messing things up?"

"I don't know," he said with sincerity. "But I'd like to find out."

Out of the corner of her eye, Jenny saw the boys making a move for the cupcakes. "Tell you what," she said to Mitch, knowing they'd be overrun in a matter of moments. "I'll stop organizing the whiteboard pens in the order of the color spectrum."

He lifted a hand to his chin and pretended to ponder. "I don't know, Jenny. Loosening the color spectrum rules? Can anarchy be far behind?"

The first of the teenage boys reached the table. "Hey, Mr. H. Jenny. Those look fantastic!"

"Help yourself, Scott." She gestured to the thick-frosted, color-sprinkled cupcakes.

"Awesome," came another boy's voice.

"You're the best!" shouted Terry.

Jenny took a step backward to avoid the fray. She could feel Mitch's gaze on her, but kept herself from looking back at him again as she headed toward the clubhouse. They'd ended their conversation on a joke. It was a lot more than she'd hoped for today.

"I can't believe things are moving along so fast," Jenny said to Emily as she peered down at several sets of house plans spread out across the glass-topped table in Cole's formal dining room.

Cole was off to one side, sprawled out in an armchair next to the open French doors, typing away on his laptop. His shirtsleeves were rolled up, and his tie loosened. "If there's going to be a change in the foundation footprint, they might as well know about it while the loaders are on site." He glanced up. "It'll save money in the long run."

"You know something about construction?" asked Emily, an edge to her voice.

"A little."

"Is there anything you don't know about?" She stared back at him with what Jenny had come to recognize as her clash-of-wills expression.

Cole paused in what looked like contemplation. "Women," he finally answered. "Specifically, you."

Jenny couldn't help but laugh.

"You're a nerd," Emily accused.

"Yeah? Well, you're dating me."

"Not after Saturday night."

"We'll see." Cole smiled confidently, going back to his work on the laptop. "You may find 12:01 comes around pretty fast. And then you'll also be dating me on Sunday."

"Conceited," Emily muttered under her breath.

"I think he's cute," Jenny whispered back.

Emily kept her voice low, leaning her head close to Jenny's. "I don't want to sleep with cute."

"Why not?" Jenny whispered back, giving Cole a surreptitious once-over. He was a very attractive man. He was in excellent physical shape. He was smart, successful, had a good sense of humor. And he was definitely one of the few males on the planet who could hold his own against Emily.

"I'm looking to get pregnant, remember?"

Ah, yes. The linebacker factor. "Would you rather sleep with Emilio?"

"Huh?"

"He's tall, brawny, definite football genes in that guy's DNA."

Emily's eyes narrowed. "Maybe. But he's kind of…I don't know. Do you think he's sexy?"

"It's not what I think that matters." Jenny thought Mitch was the one who was sexy, and look how far that had gotten her. "Who do you find sexy?"

Emily shot a fleeting, telltale glance at Cole who was typing away on his laptop. "I'm still looking," she whispered with a thread of determination.

"You two do realize I can hear you," Cole drawled.

Emily's face flushed red as she straightened in her chair. "We're not talking about you," she snapped.

"I know. You're talking about Emilio." Cole looked up again, his gaze boring deep into Emily's this time, anger lurking in the sapphire depths of his eyes.

As the tension thickened in the room, Jenny started to rise from her chair. "Why don't I just leave you two—"

"No!" Emily snapped. "Sit down. We're choosing your new house. This one." She pointed to a set of plans. "I like the contemporary hardwood floors, and all that glass."

Jenny turned her attention to the blueprints for the two-thousand square foot single-story custom house. The floor plan looked very elegant, ultramodern, with lots of planes and angles, and great circulation space between the bedrooms, kitchen and a glassed-in deck which could overlook the lake.

The front doorbell sounded, and Cole rose swiftly from his chair. Since any one of his staff members would answer, Jenny assumed it was his excuse to leave. She also didn't expect him to come back.

"Look at all those built-in closets." Emily spoke with what sounded like false cheer. "You'd have tons of room for the new wardrobe. I can picture it now, entertaining, dinner parties."

"Emily—" Jenny began.

"What?"

"This thing with Cole. Are you feeling—"

"I'm fine."

"But—"

The front door banged shut, and footsteps sounded down the hallway.

"He's coming back," said Emily. "Don't worry about it. I can handle Cole."

"...only if she's not too busy," came the sound of Mitch's voice.

Jenny stilled, her stomach clenching.

"She's in the dining room," Cole responded, and Jenny met Emily's eyes.

Emily reached out and squeezed her hand. "Are you okay?"

Jenny gave a determined nod, ignoring the butterflies circling in the pit of her stomach. "I can handle it. We spoke a few times at the office today. It was fine. I'm doing fine."

"Emily?" came Cole's voice as he appeared in the arched doorway. "Mitch needs to talk to Jenny."

Emily pivoted in her chair. "I'm not going to—"

"Emily," Cole growled. He jerked his thumb toward the hallway. "Now."

She opened her mouth, obviously about to refuse his command, but then something in his expression seemed to stop her.

"Fine," she ground out, bringing her hands down on the glass surface of the table as she rose from her chair. "But I'm not going out of earshot." She gave Jenny a significant glance. "Call me if you need me."

"I will." Jenny fought a smile. She was warmed by Emily's protective instincts. Not that they'd be remotely necessary.

Then, head held high, Emily crossed the room to Cole. Jenny noted that he put his hand on the small of her back as he ushered her out of the room.

Mitch immediately filled the empty doorway, tall, broad-shouldered, magnificently handsome as ever. She sure wished her chest wouldn't do that little hitch whenever he entered the room.

She needed to strive for equanimity. She had to stop being attracted to him. Then again, being angry with him was only marginally better. It was just as emotionally unsettling.

"Jenny." He nodded, his deep voice impacting her even more than his appearance. "Sorry to bother you after working hours."

"No problem," she automatically responded, her attention piqued. Had something gone wrong at TCC?

His gaze stopped on the paperwork in front of her.

"We were just looking at house plans," she explained.

"Pick something yet?"

Jenny shook her head. "Is everything okay at TCC?"

Mitch strode into the room, taking the chair Emily had vacated. That put him right next to Jenny, making her body respond to whatever male pheromones radiated from his pores. Her skin tingled, and her palms began to sweat.

So much for equanimity.

"I was looking for the letter to the senator. The one on the subsidies from last week."

"You couldn't find it in the directory? It should be under federal government, financial issues, political support." Jenny hated the thought that she might have misfiled something.

"Oh." He nodded. "Political support. I'll look there."

"Did you need it tonight? I can log in and get it for you. Cole probably won't mind if I use his laptop."

But Mitch was shaking his head. "I can get it in the morning."

"Okay," she agreed. But his words surprised her. If it could wait until morning, why had he gone to all the trouble to come over here?

Eight

Mitch hadn't lost the letter to the senator. He couldn't care less about the letter to the senator. All he was looking for was an excuse to come and see Jenny. She'd seemed like she was doing okay at work today, but he was still guilt-ridden over the way he'd treated her. His instinct was to apologize again. But he didn't want to belabor the issue. He supposed he wanted the best of both worlds, for Jenny to understand why they couldn't have a relationship, but for her to still like him.

Now he glanced down at the three sets of building plans. "Which way are you leaning?" he asked in an effort to keep the conversation going.

"You sure you don't need me to—"

"Don't worry about it." He waved away her question. "Tell me about your house plans."

"I haven't decided yet." She reflexively glanced down at the three drawings on the table.

Mitch swiveled the pages to face him, finding the contrast

among the three designs fascinating. It was as if completely different people had picked them out.

The first was an ultramodern contemporary, plenty of glass and sharp angles, long rooms, with sleek storage systems and display cases for art. The second was attractive, but practical. Two stories, it had three bedrooms on the top floor, a nice-sized ensuite in the master bedroom and a small balcony off the bedroom that would overlook the lake. The kitchen and dining room were L-shaped, while the living room boasted a big stone fireplace. With the exception of the skylight in the entry hall, there wasn't a lot to distinguish it from thousands of other practical houses in thousands of other residential neighborhoods around the state.

It was the third set of plans that had Mitch pondering. It was all arches and detail, softness and whimsy. It seemed to have a French provincial influence, and the demo pictures showed deep carpets, scrollwork on the wood and etching on the glass. The ceilings were high, with open beams, many of the walls were on forty-five degree angles, keeping the rooms from sitting square, while little wrought-iron balconies and bay windows gave the interior a wealth of nooks and crannies and the exterior complex detail.

He lifted one of the large sheets of blue line paper. "Did Emily pick this one?"

"Emily picked the contemporary. That one's really a token plan. You know, included so we can have three distinct choices."

"Did you pick it?"

"I did," she acknowledged.

Now Mitch was even more curious. This plan was very unlike Jenny. Well, unlike the Jenny he thought he'd known for the past year.

"Why?" he asked her.

"What do you mean?"

"I mean, out of all the thousands of house plans in all the world, why choose this one as a top three pick?"

There was a definite note of defensiveness in Jenny's tone as she responded. "I wanted to look at something completely different."

"I like it," he said.

"I find it impractical." She pointed to the living room, the dining room and one of the bedrooms. "How could you possibly arrange furniture in there?"

"I guess you'd turn it on an angle. Or have something custom designed." He pointed to an alcove in the kitchen. "You could put a half-octagonal breakfast nook in there. Or a window seat and a planter. There are a thousand things—"

"I don't know why I even added it to the list." Her lips compressed into a line, and she folded her hands primly in her lap.

He covered her hands with his own. "I'm not your mother, Jenny."

"What is that supposed to mean?" She pulled herself free.

"It means, you're allowed to like something, just because you like it. You don't need an excuse, and it doesn't always need to be functional, practical and utilitarian."

"I'm not about to build an impractical house."

"I would," said Mitch, meaning it. He'd build whatever house struck his fancy. And he'd build it in the blink of an eye if Jenny wanted it.

He gave his head a shake, chasing away that ridiculous thought. Jenny's taste was irrelevant when it came to his house.

"Those bay windows all add cost," she told him. "They'll be a pain to clean, and I can't afford custom furniture."

"You'll have the insurance settlement to spend."

She gave him a sharp glance. "You know what I mean."

"What if you had an unlimited budget?"

"I don't."

"Play along with me for a second. *If* you had an unlimited budget?"

She mulishly set her jaw.

But he waited her out.

"Fine," she capitulated, pointing to the French country plans. "If I had an unlimited budget, I'd add a big deck out back over-looking the lake, and a turret up front." She moved her finger. "Right there. With a round room on the top floor that had window seating all round. I'd buy dozens of pillows and cur-tains with ruffles, in a floral pattern that looked like a country garden. It would have deep, cushy seats, and a thick green carpet."

"Green?"

"Like grass. And everything would be soft."

He took in her rosy cheeks, the pout of her mouth, the moss green of her eyes and the way her dark lashes slowly stroked with each blink. "Soft is nice."

"This is ridiculous. I don't know how you talked me into daydreaming." She shook her head, moving back, appearing to physically distance herself from the whimsical house plans.

He continued to study her expression. As usual, his desire for her battled its way to the surface. But it was tempered this time, tempered by something warm, something soft and protective. His voice went husky. "It's not ridiculous to have dreams."

She twisted her head to look at him. "A person should stay away from dreams that have no hope of coming true."

On impulse, he smoothed a stray lock of her hair back, tucking it behind one ear. "Those are the only kind worth having."

She rubbed her cheek where his hand had touched it. "Really? So, what are your dreams, Mitch?"

It was impossible for him to answer. Because right then, he was toying with a dream that involved Jenny and forever.

He took a safe answer. "I want to play professional football."

But she shook her head. "Come on, Mitch. That's not a dream. That was already your reality. We're playing a game. You have to come up with something you could never have in a million years."

He searched his brain for an acceptable answer and ended

up stalling. "I don't know, Jenny. There aren't a lot of things I can't buy."

"Something money can't buy."

"Happiness?"

"Sure." She waited for him to elaborate.

This time, he tried to be honest. "I want the TCC to have a successful election that brings the membership together under a good leader."

She rolled her eyes. "Lame."

"You don't want that?"

"Of course I want it. But that's motherhood and apple pie. Who doesn't want it? Plus, it's not for you personally. Tell me something that's for you."

"I can't think of anything off the top of my head."

"Oh, yes, you can." She was obviously not going to let this go. "I owned up to secretly wanting a silly, whimsical house. Spill."

"You should build that house."

"Quit stalling."

But he had to stall, because he knew exactly what it was that would make him happy. Something he could dream about and never have. But he wasn't going to tell Jenny. He refused to hurt her all over again.

He shook his head. "I can't tell you."

"Yes, you can."

"No, I really can't." Inside his head, he was asking himself what the hell he thought he was doing even flirting with the truth. He needed a lie, and he needed one quick.

"Why not?" she pressed.

"Let it go."

"You wouldn't let me off the hook."

He thought about it for a moment longer. And then he gave her a different truth. "I want a miracle cure for my shoulder. I want to be back to one hundred percent."

"You will be—"

But he shook his head. "I keep telling myself it's getting better." He hadn't voiced his deep-seated fear out loud to anyone. He didn't really know why he was doing it now. "But it's not."

She reached out and touched his arm, her sympathies obviously engaged. "You just have to be patient."

"This isn't about patience. It's about the physical limitations on the human body." Now that he'd stuck his toe in the pool of bald honesty, he plunged all the way under. "I see the expression on the physiotherapist's face, the expression on my doctor's face. They told me six months. Well, it's been a year. And there's been no discernable progress for the last six weeks."

"I understand these things can plateau."

He sent her a look that told her to stop lying.

She swallowed. "That's your secret dream?"

"Yes." It was the only secret dream he could tell her about. The other was a relationship between the two of them where she didn't get hurt in the end. Impossible.

"Is there anything I can do to help?" she asked.

The genuine caring in her eyes blew him away. After all that had happened, all he'd done to her, that she could muster up this kind of compassion for him was nothing short of amazing.

"Anybody ever tell you you're a saint?"

She coughed out a laugh. "Good grief, no. My mother used to tell me I was the devil in disguise."

"Your mother had no right to say that."

"She was ill."

"She was nasty."

Jenny gave a philosophical shrug. "She's out of the state now, and out of my day-to-day life."

On impulse, Mitch brushed the pad of his index finger across Jenny's temple. "Don't let her live on up here."

"I'm not."

"Build the house, Jenny. The one you love."

"Are you going to pay for it?"

It took everything Mitch had not to say yes.

* * *

Wednesday evening, Jenny determinedly rolled up the plans for the French country house and slid them into a cardboard tube. It was all well and good for Mitch to tell her to dream. But reality was reality. She wasn't building it.

"Jenny?" Cole called from the front room. He was home earlier than usual, and she hadn't heard him come in.

"Back here," she answered in response, tucking the plans to the back of a shelf on his built-in china cabinet.

Cole had been incredibly generous about letting her stay with him. She was becoming positively spoiled by the cook and the housekeeper, and she now teased him about never leaving.

He'd told her she was welcome to stay as long as she liked. He said he'd begun to think of her as the sister he'd never had. Since Jenny had always wanted siblings of her own, his words had touched her on a very deep, emotional level.

He strode into the dining room, loosening his tie, having already discarded his suit jacket somewhere along the way. "Can I ask you a huge favor?" He winked and grinned. "Sis?"

"Am I going to hate this?" she teased in return.

"I hope not. You can say no if you really hate it."

"What if I only sort of hate it?"

"Then you should say yes and make me happy."

"Go ahead." She pretended to brace herself against the back of a chair. "Hit me with it."

"Jeffrey Porter called today. From the Tigers."

"I know who you mean."

"He offered a fifty-thousand-dollar contribution to my hospital charity if I gave him my fourth ticket for the Longhorn Banquet."

The fourth ticket? So, he'd be attending with them.

"He'd be my date?" Jenny asked.

"He would. Tickets have been sold out for months."

Jenny didn't have anything against Jeffrey. She didn't see her and Jeffrey going anywhere on the relationship front. But fifty thousand dollars was a lot of money.

"It's a good charity?" she asked Cole.

"They're building a new pediatric wing."

"He won't think he and I are on a real date, right?"

Cole shook his head.

Jenny analyzed the request for a downside. It was a lost opportunity to date someone new. Then again, there'd be a whole lot of new people at the party.

"What do you think?" Cole put in.

"As long as you don't think I'll be misleading him."

"Don't worry. He just broke up with his girlfriend. But he's not looking for a replacement. Trust me when I tell you you're not going to break Jeffrey's heart."

"That did sound kind of conceited, didn't it?"

"It sounded very sweet. You're a caring person, Jenny Watson."

"And so are you."

"You'll tell Emily that?"

"I already have."

"I like having you in my corner, sis."

"And I like having you in mine." She hesitated. "Bro." Then she giggled. "I've never called anyone that in my life."

"Then, I stand adopted. Did you pick out a dress yet?"

She shook her head. "I was thinking about going to look for something tonight." She made a show of inhaling the spicy aroma of the cook's baking lasagna. "After dinner."

Cole reached into the pocket of his slacks. "Here, take my credit card."

"Don't be ridiculous." Jenny might not be able to afford custom furniture, but she could definitely afford her own clothes.

He flipped open his leather wallet. "I want you to get something special."

"I'm not taking your credit card, Cole."

He seemed to be ignoring her. "In fact, why don't you call Emily. Go to Maximillians. Tell her I'm buying for you both."

Jenny felt her jaw drop open. "*The* Maximillians?"

Had he lost his mind? The purses alone at that store cost three thousand dollars.

But he held out the slim platinum credit card. "If you don't let me buy a dress for you, Emily will never let me buy one for her."

"You can't spend that kind of— You can't spend *any* kind of money on our dresses."

"But I can. That's one of the perks of making a whole lot of money. You get to spend it on anything you want."

"I'm saying no, Cole." She took a backward step. There was no way he was talking her into doing this.

He stepped forward. "I *need* you to do this."

"You don't—"

"Correct me if I'm wrong, but I think Emily might, just might, be slightly attracted to me."

Slightly attracted? Jenny was pretty sure it was a lot more than slightly attracted. She also realized Emily was fighting it for all she was worth.

"I want to see what she'll do. If she has the chance to pick out a dress, a no-holds-barred, money-is-no-object dress, just for a date with me, I really need to know what it is she'll choose. Do me this favor, sis."

Jenny rolled her eyes. "I can't believe it." She socked Cole playfully on the shoulder. "I cannot believe you just made the one and only argument that could get me to use your credit card to buy a three thousand dollar dress."

"Don't restrict yourself to three thousand." Cole grinned. "And don't restrict yourself to a dress. You're going to need shoes and accessories. And so will Emily."

Jenny continued to shake her head. This was surreal.

He took her hand and placed the credit card firmly in her

palm. "I mean it. You have to go wild. If you do it, Emily will do it, and then I'll know whether or not I've got a shot."

"She might just spend your money out of spite," Jenny felt compelled to warn him. While she was pretty sure Emily harbored a secret attraction to Cole, she was also sure Emily had a very strong will. She didn't want to fall for Cole, and she was annoyed at him for chasing her.

"I won't get my answer because she spends my money. I'll get my answer from what she spends it on."

The edges of the credit card were hard against Jenny's palm. "Are you sure about this?"

"I am positive about this. Call her. Right now."

Jenny tucked the credit card away and reached for her phone. "What are you hoping she'll buy?"

Cole gave a shrug. "I'll know it when I see it."

Jenny pressed her speed dial. Then she listened to Emily's gasp of disbelief, followed by her growing conviction that Jenny should absolutely indulge herself at Cole's expense and, finally, her mounting excitement as she bought fully into the plan.

Mitch had watched Jenny drive off from Cole's house half an hour ago, so he knew Cole would be alone. He knew he had no one but himself to blame, but he missed the days of being able to wander over to Cole's house on a whim, or having Cole wander over to his house to share the interesting bits of information from their lives. It never had to be earth-shattering, not the kind of thing where you pick up the phone to call your family or whoop it up with the gang, just the everyday, normal things that you wanted to share with another human being.

But he felt like he couldn't invade Jenny's space every evening. So, instead, now Cole was with Jenny, while Mitch was alone. He felt as if he'd screwed up two relationships in his life.

As he started up the driveway, Cole came out the front door, car keys in his hand, striding toward his Mustang.

"Hey, Cole," Mitch called out, in case Cole hadn't spotted him.

It appeared he hadn't, because he turned guiltily. "Oh, hey, Mitch."

"Got a hot date?" Mitch joked, striding closer.

"No. I'm..." He pocketed the keys. "It's nothing." He hesitated a moment longer. "You up for a beer?"

"I don't want to hold you up."

"No. Not at all. No big deal."

"Where were you going?" Mitch couldn't help but ask. It wasn't like Cole to act all twitchy like this.

"Errands. Come on." Cole turned back for the house. "I've got a couple of lagers on ice."

Feeling vaguely like an interloper, Mitch followed along. "I got some news a few days ago." For some reason he felt like he ought to get straight to the point.

"Good news?" asked Cole as they made their way through the house.

"Pretty good."

Cole reached for the refrigerator door.

"I've been short-listed for the Youth Outreach Award at the Longhorn Banquet."

Cole's reach faltered. "On Saturday?"

"Yeah." What other Longhorn Banquet was there in Texas?

There was something wrong with Cole. "And you just found out?"

"Last week, actually. But with everything that's been going on, I didn't want to...you know, intrude over here."

Cole swung open the door, his voice hearty. "That's great. Congratulations, buddy." He snagged two bottles and pressed one into Mitch's hand.

"What's wrong?" Mitch had known Cole way too long to fall for this act.

"Nothing's wrong."

Now Mitch was getting mad. It was one thing to be ostracized by Jenny. He deserved that. But he was still Cole's friend. "What the hell?"

"Fine." Cole twisted off the cap. "I had four tickets. So I invited Emily. And Jeffrey is taking Jenny."

Mitch felt as though someone had punched him in the solar plexus. "You're double-dating?"

Cole nodded, then took a swig of the beer.

"With Jenny and *Jeffrey?*"

"Yes."

"Son of a bitch."

"Me?"

"No. Jeffrey. I'm assuming you're just trying to get into Emily's pants."

Cole frowned. "That's not exactly what I had—"

"*You* didn't know I'd be there. I get that. But Jeffrey." Mitch's anger bubbled boldly to the surface.

He'd told himself a thousand times that Jenny was allowed to date anyone she wanted. He'd forfeited his right to an opinion a couple of weeks back. But he'd warned Jeffrey away. He'd warned Jeffrey in no uncertain terms that he was to stay away from Jenny.

"Jeffrey knew you'd be there?" For some reason, that revelation made Cole smile.

"Don't you dare laugh."

"He's messin' with you, Mitch."

"Of course he's messin' with me. I told him to stay away from her. I warned him not to hurt her."

Cole looked like he had something more to say. But instead, he took the bottle of beer back from Mitch and placed them both on the granite countertop. "I sent them shopping."

"Who?"

"Emily and Jenny. I gave them my credit card and sent them to Maximillians to buy dresses for the banquet."

That didn't sound right. "Jenny won't spend your money."

"That's where I was headed when you showed up just now," Cole responded. "To make sure she did."

"You were going to Maximillians?"

"I was."

"I'm coming, too." Mitch pivoted to head for the front door. "And you're not buying Jenny a dress."

"Yes, I am."

"No, *I* am."

The thread of a chuckle was back in Cole's voice. "Why does that not surprise me?"

Mitch turned to glare at his friend.

"And good luck with that," Cole added.

Mitch didn't need luck. He was a professional football player. He had strength, guts, agility and endless determination. He'd already defied the odds nine ways to Sunday. He could get one woman to buy one single dress. And since it was for a date with Jeffrey, he'd push for something that went from wrists to ankles, no cleavage, preferably in a sedate gray woolen blend.

By the time they arrived at Maximillians, Mitch had decided on exactly the dress Jenny should wear. But when he entered the store and made his way to the changing area, honing in on the sounds of Jenny and Emily's voices, the nun outfit flew right from his head.

Jenny stood in front of the three-way mirror in a black strapless sheath of a full-length dress that flared out at the knees. The top was sequined and dipped low between her breasts, clinging like a second skin.

His mouth went dry, and his knees went weak.

"You'll have all the men at the gala panting after you like Labrador retrievers." Emily laughed.

That was Mitch's fear, too.

Emily was dressed in a short, full-skirted deep-blue satin dress. It was also strapless, and flared from the waist to reveal a black crinoline peeking out at the hem.

Mitch felt Cole come to a halt beside him.

Jenny gazed wide-eyed at herself in the mirror and seemed to stumble for words. "It's too…too…"

Too *everything,* Mitch wanted to shout. If she was dating

him, sure, it was a perfect dress. But not when she was dating Jeffrey.

"Perhaps the silver?" a sales clerk offered, holding up a slinky, short dress with capped sleeves and ties that crisscrossed the open back.

Jenny frowned at it uncertainly.

"I'll try that one," Emily put in, scooping the hanger from the sales clerk.

"Go with the blue," Cole muttered under his breath.

"Can you grab me some shoes?" Emily called as she pulled the heavy curtain shut.

"Sure." Jenny turned and immediately spotted Mitch. Her jaw dropped open, and she glanced to the right and to the left, as if looking for the punch line to a joke.

She made her way toward him, every movement sinuous and graceful. Her voice, however, was an accusatory hiss. "What are you doing here?"

"He came with me," Cole put in, and Jenny seemed to notice Cole for the first time.

"Why?"

"I got curious," said Cole. "I couldn't wait to see what she picked out."

"I meant why did you bring Mitch?"

"We were having a beer."

Jenny compressed her lips.

"I won't get in the way," Mitch found himself promising.

"I'm going to ignore you," Jenny announced.

"Fair enough. Do you want to know what I think of that dress?"

She glared at him. "Absolutely not."

"Okay," he agreed.

But when she stared at him a moment longer, he found his gaze dropping to the cleavage, to the nipped-in waist and to the clingy fabric where it hugged her hips.

"You don't like it," she stated.

"That's not the problem."

"Then what's the problem? You're grimacing."

"That style isn't you."

"It is now." She brushed past him. "I have to get Emily some silver shoes."

"Get her a bag, too," called Cole, and Jenny cracked what looked like a reluctant grin as she shook her head.

Mitch watched as she made her way across the store. She consulted with the shoe salesman, chose two pairs, then started back. On the way, she paused at a rack, taking out something gauzy and pastel, her expression softening as she ran her fingers over the fabric. But when the sales clerk approached her with two more dresses, she let the gauzy one fall back on the rack. The two women chatted on their way back to the changing area.

Curious, Mitch went to see what had caught her eye.

He couldn't have been more surprised. It was a V-necked, spaghetti-strapped dress made of pale, mottled rainbow silk. The soft, romantic colors were very unlike Jenny, as was the swish of the layered skirt that came to points at the hem, and the tiny jewels that adorned the neck and the waist.

For some reason, the dress reminded him of the house plans. Did Jenny have a secret romantic side? Instead of geometric lines and practicality, did she truly long for swirls and irreverence? The idea intrigued him.

"Hand-painted," came the clerk's voice from behind his shoulder. "One of my favorite designers. Brand-new in today. Is it for someone special?"

Mitch was willing to bet every item in the store was made by one of the clerk's favorite designers. But if this particular one had caught Jenny's eye, he wanted to see her in it.

He nodded to the changing rooms. "Can you take it to the woman who's trying things on? The one with the strawberry blond hair?"

"Of course." The clerk smiled, removing the dress from the display.

"Don't tell her it's from me."

The woman touched her finger to her lips to promise her silence, and Mitch gave her a nod of appreciation.

He moved to another section of the store, pretending to ignore Jenny. In his peripheral vision, he caught her puzzled frown and her initial head shake to the clerk. But the persistent clerk prevailed, and Jenny took the dress into her cubical.

Mitch made his way casually back to the changing area.

"Are you going to offer an opinion?" Emily was demanding of Cole as she modeled the silver dress. "Or just stand there and gawk?"

"I'm here to make sure you don't go overboard with my credit card."

"Oh, I'm going overboard all right." She held out one of her silver sandaled feet. "See these? They're Amerelda, three-inch heels, and I'm buying them."

"What about the blue dress?"

"You liked the blue dress?"

"Your choice."

"Well, I like them both."

"Then buy them both."

Emily put her nose in the air as she flounced off. "I think I will."

Mitch turned to Cole and raised his brows, wondering if his friend had a master plan. "This is going to be an awfully expensive date."

"Like I care."

Mitch considered Cole's determined expression, and came to the simple conclusion that he had it very, very bad for Emily Kiley. In a misery-loves-company way, it made him feel better. But only by a very small margin.

"I hope she's worth it," he offered to Cole.

"I figure I'll know by the end of the weekend."

Then Jenny appeared in the hand-painted silk, and the breath left Mitch's body. She looked like a goddess, a fairy nymph who wandered out of a mystical garden. The colors set off her honey-toned skin, meshing perfectly with her minimal makeup and her delicate features. Her limbs were long and graceful, and he immediately pictured her with wild flowers in her hair, tiny white satin sandals and a trailing bouquet.

He found his feet moving, taking him closer to where she swayed one way then the other in front of the mirror. The words *buy it, buy it, buy it* echoed through his head, but he kept himself determinedly silent.

"It's really not me," she said to no one in particular.

Mitch moved closer still. "Pretend for a minute," he said softly. "That you're not you."

"Well, that's ridiculous." But she smiled as she said it, and a warmth invaded his system.

"It goes with your eyes," he offered, easing closer still, turning the conversation more intimate.

"It would have to. There's every color in the universe on this."

"Do you like it?"

"Maybe if I was a fairy princess. But I'd never wear it again."

"So what?"

"I'm not going to buy a dress this expensive to wear once."

"I'll buy it for you," Mitch found himself vowing. Then he instantly regretted the words when her smile disappeared.

"Cole told me his plan," Mitch quickly amended, backpedaling fast. "I only meant that anything that won't fit on his credit card will fit on mine. Don't you want to be a fairy princess for just one night?"

A longing burned deep in Jenny's green eyes, and he knew in that instant she was the fairy princess. She'd been the cautious, perfect child for her mother, the professional, meticulous employee at the TCC, and the chic, sophisticated city girl for Emily, but deep down inside, Jenny wanted to be the princess.

She needed this dress. And she needed the whimsical house and the custom furniture. And Mitch vowed to himself that he would move heaven and earth to make those things happen for her.

Suddenly, Emily appeared from her change room, and her eyes went wide when she saw Jenny. "Wow. That's sure not you."

"It's not, is it?" And some of the light went out of Jenny's eyes.

Cole moved closer to stand next to Mitch.

"But isn't that the point?" Mitch quickly put in, feeling almost desperate. "For Jenny to buy something completely different? When is she going to get a chance like this again? It's hand-painted silk," he parroted the sales clerk. "Just came into the store today. One of her—" he gestured vaguely to the clerk across the store "—favorite designers."

Both Jenny and Emily blinked at him in surprise.

"I overheard," he defended.

Emily took another look at the dress. "Well, maybe," she allowed.

"Once in a lifetime," Mitch repeated. Then he lowered his voice for Jenny's ears alone. "A dream."

Jenny hesitated for a long moment. Then she turned back to the mirror. She pivoted, letting the skirt swirl around her thighs.

"It'll look great on the dance floor," Mitch dared. "You need some white satin sandals, low heels, maybe a ribbon at the ankle."

"What the hell's up with you?" Cole muttered beside him.

"Shut up."

"That might look good," said Emily. "Really, what the heck?"

Jenny smiled, and Mitch's chest went tight. It was a perfectly natural reaction, he assured himself. He'd never claimed that he didn't admire Jenny, only that he wasn't any good for her. He wanted her to be happy. She deserved it.

Nine

The awards had been handed out by the governor, the speeches made, dinner was finished and Mitch's distinguished plaque for the Youth Outreach Award was parked with the others on a table for attendees to admire. As the best days in Mitch's life went, this would probably rank as the worst.

He'd made it through his short speech, thanking all the right people, but all he could see was that Jenny was with Jeffrey instead of him. And echoing inside his brain were his doctor's words from earlier this morning. His worst fear had been realized today. Mitch was never going to play football again.

He hadn't said a word to anyone, and now he was standing on the sidelines as the dancing began, accepting congratulations from friends, acquaintances and strangers while watching Jenny in Jeffrey's arms.

He should have talked her into the gray wool blend instead of the rainbow silk after all. He resented the way the delicate dress flowed around her sexy legs, a splash of color in a sea of monochrome. Her hair was styled in a crown of braids, wisps flowing free over her temples and along her neck. And she'd found a pair of white silk sandals. The heels were higher than he'd pictured, but they were strappy and delicate, rhinestones winking around her slim ankles.

She was perfect, and it was all for another man.

He took a deep drink of his single malt.

She disappeared from his view, and he reflexively shifted, nearly knocking into an older gentleman in a tux, who scowled at Mitch, his bushy brows drawing together. Mitch gave a perfunctory apology, not particularly caring that the man might be someone important.

He wove his way through the crowd, trying to come to terms with the fact that he wasn't a pro football player anymore. What was he now? Just a guy with a nest egg and no career, whose services would soon not even be required at the TCC. They'd have a new president, and Mitch would have little to do and nothing of value to contribute to the community.

He came closer to the edge of the dance floor, telling himself to stop wallowing in self-pity. But watching Jenny laugh in Jeffrey's arms made everything that much worse. Jeffrey should let go of her. He needed to let go of her right now. In Mitch's raw, emotional state, he needed Jenny in *his* arms, not in his teammate's.

Scratch that. He and Jeffrey weren't teammates anymore.

Mitch stuck his glass on an empty tray stand as the music changed from one song to the next. The band was sticking to classics, with the occasional jazz tune tossed in. No pop and no rock, and apparently no country, even though this was Texas.

When the floral arrangements were two feet high, the main course was Kobe beef and Newfoundland lobster, and the average carat weight per woman was in the low double digits, he supposed Keith Urban was out of the question. Still, he had an urge to scoop Jenny up, get rid of his bow tie and jacket, and head for the nearest honky-tonk where they could kick back.

He craned his neck, scanning the floor. Where had she gone?

"Having a good time so far?" came Jeffrey's deep voice.

"A blast," Mitch responded drily, determinedly swallowing his misery, bracing himself for an up close view of Jenny in the dress. But when he turned his head, she wasn't with Jeffrey.

"She's out on the dance floor." Jeffrey had correctly interpreted Mitch's expression.

"You left her there alone?" That was even worse.

"She's got a new partner."

"Who?" Mitch demanded.

Jeffrey chuckled. "I didn't get his name."

Mitch strained to look, but couldn't catch a glimpse of her dress. "You didn't tell her I was going to be here, did you?"

"Was I supposed to tell her that?" Jeffrey accepted a glass of wine from a passing waiter.

Mitch declined another drink. "I saw her expression of shock when my name was called at the podium."

"Yet she wasn't sitting anywhere close to you."

"Don't get cute. I thought you would have given her a heads-up is all." Mitch took a step back to get out of the line of circulation around the dance floor.

"Why didn't you tell her yourself?"

"I barely saw her this week." Except in the office. And in the office, they were being careful to stick to business.

"She told me about the dress," said Jeffrey.

"That was Cole."

"Cole said it was you."

"Cole has a big mouth." Mitch changed his mind about the wine and caught the next waiter who came by.

"So, why are you turning yourself inside out watching me dance with her?"

Mitch grunted a noncommittal answer. So he didn't want Jenny at the mercy of a player like Jeffrey. That was simply good taste.

"You don't want to date her," Jeffrey pointed out, watching Mitch a little too closely.

"Of course I don't want to date her. But I don't want you to date her, either."

"Noble sentiment. If you were her father, and if this was the nineteenth century."

"Ha, ha," Mitch mocked.

"Seriously, Mitch. Am I making my point out there?" He cocked his head to the dance floor. "You need to either start dating her yourself or step aside."

"I already stepped aside."

"The hell you did. You haven't taken your eyes off her all night."

"I can't see her now."

"She's to the left of the band."

Mitch zeroed in. He felt a little buzz of relief at seeing her proper stance with her dance partner. He could live with those six inches of airspace between them. But he wasn't so crazy about the guy's expression, nor about the way he kept glancing at her cleavage.

"Tell me something, Mitch."

"Yeah?"

"That guy she's dancing with? What do you want to do to him?"

"Rip his head off and kick it through the uprights."

"I rest my case."

"You have no case."

"You can't take out every guy who wants to sleep with her. Because take a good look at her, Mitch, lots of guys are going to want to sleep with her."

"It better not frickin' be you."

"It'll never be me."

Mitch didn't trust that promise, not one little bit. "Why not?"

"Because you're my friend, and because I know what's going on here."

For a split second, Mitch thought Jeffrey meant his shoulder injury. But he quickly realized it was impossible for Jeffrey to know what the doctor had said.

"What's going on here?" Mitch asked.

"What's going on here is that you've been sacked one too many times behind the line of scrimmage, and it's resulted in serious brain damage. Otherwise, you'd be out there on that dance floor with Jenny. She's incredible, Mitch. And she said she wants to date you. But, oh, no, you're so busy protecting your dating future with generic blonde bombshells, that you—"

"That's not what this is about," Mitch growled.

Jeffrey snorted. "The hell it's not."

"Give me one reason why I should take advice from you."

"Because I screwed up. I had my chance with Celeste, and I blew it. I have to start all over again." His voice went lower. "You watched me screw up, so now you don't have to."

"It's not that simple," said Mitch, even as his thigh muscles quivered with the need to cross the hall to Jenny. He tried to tell himself it wasn't fair to Jenny to date her. But a growing chorus in his brain kept telling him he wouldn't hurt her. He liked her too much to ever let himself hurt her. He honestly didn't know which side of the argument to believe anymore.

"Song's about to change," Jeffrey warned.

Mitch swore under his breath. Giving in, he took the first few steps toward the dance floor.

Mitch was heading her way. Jenny watched him weave through the crowd on the dance floor. His gaze had locked on hers, and his jaw was set to a determined angle, shoulders square, stride eating up the distance between them. Judging by the flare in his blue eyes, he was either going to ask her to dance or have her arrested.

The strains of the music faded around her, and she relaxed her hold on her partner, stepping away.

"Thank you." She smiled and nodded to the man she'd just met, drawing away and switching her attention back to Mitch.

She drew a little hitch of a breath, letting her arms fall to her sides and reflexively moistening her lips. She felt pretty tonight in a way she never had before. It was the dress, the hairstyle, the subtle makeup and the delicate shoes. And there was no denying, it was also the way men regarded her.

Normally, she caught very few eyes. At the wedding and the football party, when she'd been dressed in such sophisticated clothes, their interest had been frankly sexual. But tonight was different. There was respect in their eyes, a deference in their tone when they asked for a dance.

Jenny smiled to herself, thinking she could get used to this.

Mitch was thirty feet away now. She definitely wasn't seeing deference in his expression. Still, she found herself eagerly anticipating his arrival.

Would he ask her to dance? Would she say yes? What would happen when she was in his arms again? Would all her well-laid plans fly out the window? Because the one thing she definitely could not achieve with Mitch was equanimity.

He came to a halt in front of her.

Neither of them spoke, but his expression softened.

"I like your dress," he finally spoke.

"Thank you."

The music came up again, and she felt self-conscious standing still in the middle of the swaying couples.

"Did you want to dance?" she asked him, taking away her option to say no. Not that she realistically thought she'd say no to him.

"No," he told her, making her feel more self-conscious than ever. "I want to get out of here," he finished.

She wasn't sure how to take that. Was he saying goodbye? She couldn't control a wash of disappointment.

He steadily held her gaze. "Come with me."

Yes, yes, yes. "I came here with Jeffrey," she reluctantly replied. "I can't just leave him."

But Mitch took her hand, something that looked like pain

filtering through his eyes. "Only as far as the grounds. I've got to get away from this crowd for a few minutes."

"Is something wrong?" She couldn't imagine why Mitch would feel a need to leave. He was a celebrity tonight. She'd been surreptitiously watching him while she danced, and he'd had a steady stream of congratulations, everyone from the governor to movie stars.

"Yeah," he told her, towing her along. "Something's wrong."

He shouldered his way through the crowd, her hand still firmly clasped in his as he cleared a path to the bank of French doors that led to a huge concrete veranda.

It was a warm, humid night, and a few couples were engaged in conversation around the lighted deck, drinks in hand, dresses sparkling along with the laughter.

Mitch glanced around, then headed for the stairs that led down to the gardens and manicured lawn of the River Bend Club.

Clouds had obscured the moon, and the only illumination came from the windows of the club behind them, discrete pot lighting in the gardens and the residential buildings far across the river.

At the bottom of the stairs, her heels sank into the soft grass. "Wait," she gasped.

He abruptly stopped, turning.

"My—" She shook her hand free from his, lifting her feet one at a time and peeling off her sandals and dangling them from one hand. "How far are we going?"

He gazed out ahead of them. "I don't know. Until we're away." His voice was stark, his jaw clenched, his eyes slate gray.

"Mitch, what's wrong?" She was getting worried.

"Do you mind if we walk?"

"Of course not." She fell into step, glancing up at his profile every few feet, wondering if he was going to tell her why he was upset.

Finally, she couldn't stand it anymore. "What's going on, Mitch. Has somebody been hurt?"

"Yeah." His voice was flat.

Oh, no. "Who?"

"Me."

"What?" She froze. "How?"

He halted and turned back to face her, voice hoarse. "I spoke to the team doctor today. It's official. I'm never going to play football again."

Jenny's stomach sank. "No," she rasped.

It wasn't possible. He'd worked so hard. He'd done everything they'd told him to do. He had the best physiotherapist, the best surgeons. He was young and fit and incredibly healthy.

"Are you sure?"

"Yes."

"I mean, is there—"

His voice went raw. "You don't think I asked them to double-check? To triple-check? To call Sweden and see if there was a new procedure or a miracle cure?"

Of course he'd done all that. What a stupid, stupid question.

"It's done, Jenny." Now, his voice was devoid of emotion. "It's over. I'm thirty years old, and my career is finished."

"Oh, Mitch." She blinked back the sting of tears, swallowing hard as her throat closed in.

Mitch's gaze went to the brightly lit castlelike building behind her. "I'm sorry. I didn't mean to be selfish and drag you into this. You should get back inside."

"But—"

"Jeffrey's waiting."

"Jeffrey will understand."

"I wouldn't."

She stepped boldly forward. "I'm not leaving you."

"I don't deserve that."

It didn't matter what he deserved or didn't deserve. There

was no way she was leaving him right now. "Do you need to yell? Scream? Get it out of your system?"

"I'm not going to yell at you."

"You can," she offered.

"It's not your fault."

"That doesn't matter. If you need to—"

He reached out to her, gently grasping her upper arm. "Stop. You are *not* going to be my whipping post."

"I am so sorry, Mitch." She placed a hand on his chest, feeling his heat, feeling his heartbeat, wishing there was something she could do to help.

"Jenny, don't."

But she stepped into the touch and pressed more firmly. "You don't deserve this, Mitch."

He gave a weak laugh. "And you don't deserve the likes of me."

"I don't have you," she pointed out.

"Don't you?" His deep gaze bore into hers.

He trapped her hand, squeezing it tight against his hard chest, his voice hollow and haunted. "I try and I try. But I can't seem to stay away."

The shoes slipped from her fingertips, landing softly on the lawn below. Before she could censor them, her feelings whispered out. "Then stop trying."

Her voice was deep and throaty. And she realized she didn't want to censor the words. She meant them with all her heart.

She shifted closer still, her breasts brushing the back of his hand. If there was a small measure of comfort she could give him, even if it was only temporary, she was willing.

His chest heaved.

She walked her fingers up the front of his dress shirt, stopping at the black bow tie.

"We can't," he strained.

"We can," she countered. "In fact, we already have."

He trapped her wandering hand once more. "This will only make it worse."

She swore she could feel his hurt throbbing tight in his chest. She couldn't bear to leave him. "Or, it might make it better."

"And if it ends?" he rasped. "When it ends?"

"When it ends, I'll survive. You said it yourself, Mitch. Everything in my life doesn't have to be planned, controlled and logical. Deep down inside, I'm impulsive and wild."

He groaned her name.

"Let me be impulsive and wild."

His hand convulsed over hers, tugging it tight against his chest, the blue flame of his gaze heating her through to the core.

"I wish I could make a guarantee," he rasped.

She smiled serenely, certain of her decision. "I don't want a guarantee."

All the way back to his hotel suite, Mitch expected Jenny to change her mind, or else to evaporate from his dream, leaving him to wake up alone, sweating and frustrated in a tangle of sheets.

But she didn't.

And he closed the suite door behind them, leaning back against it as the latch clicked into place. He watched her walk across the plush carpet, into the dimly lit sitting area.

"You forgot your shoes," he pointed out.

She turned. "You want to go back?"

He shook his head, stepping forward, tugging the loose end of his bow tie and tossing it on a chair. His tux jacket followed as he moved toward her. He was about to make the biggest mistake of his life, but he couldn't bring himself to care. He was too raw with emotional pain, too tired of fighting his feelings for Jenny. He didn't have it in him to be strong. Reality would to have to wait for tomorrow.

He reached out to touch her face, stroking his rough fingertips along the smooth satin of her cheek. "How is it possible for you to be so beautiful?"

Her smile widened, green eyes glowing jade.

He cupped her ear, the back of her neck, bending and drawing her close. His lips touched hers, and his eyes closed shut in response to her sweet taste, the moist heat of her mouth.

He wrapped an arm around her waist, drawing her close and feeling her lithe curves mold against him. She fit so perfectly. Though he fought for control, and he strained to take this slow, raw desire throbbed its way insistently into his system. His kisses grew harder, longer, deeper. His skin caught fire, and his muscles turned to tempered steel.

She met his tongue, and he bent her backward, his hand roaming from her neck, to her shoulder, along the side of her breast, whispering over the thin silk that covered her body. From the second he saw her in this dress, he'd longed to feel her heat through the gossamer fabric.

His palm rounded her buttocks, pressing her against his taut thighs. He groaned as the soft curve of her belly came up against him.

She clung to his shoulders, while he kissed her temple, her ear, her neck, skipping over the jeweled trim of her dress to press his hot lips against the smooth honey-tone of her shoulder.

Her lips touched his chest, kissing him through the pressed fabric of his shirt. For some reason, the gesture seemed intensely erotic, and he threw back his head to savor the sensation. Her fingers fumbled with his buttons then. She kissed his bare chest, and lust ricocheted from his brain to his toes and all points in between.

He scooped her into his arms, capturing her swollen mouth with his own, kissing her hard while she cradled his head, curling her body against him. He strode for the bedroom, ignoring the light switch, navigating by the dim glow of the city lights that filtered through the gauzy curtains.

He lowered himself to the bed, falling backward onto the

thick quilt, pulling her down on top of him and running his hands up the back of her thighs, finding the lace of her tiny panties, then drawing her softness more solidly against him.

Between hot kisses, she pushed off his shirt. He pulled down the zipper at the back of her dress. But she drew back and shook her head, catching her bottom lip with her white teeth. Her hair had come loose from the braids, and her eyes simmered with deep desire.

He forced his hands to still. He'd be as patient as she needed, even though it might kill him. To his surprise, she rolled the lace panties down the length of her legs, tossing them aside. Then she pulled upright, sitting astride him.

"Is this what you pictured?" she asked in a throaty voice. "Was this your fantasy?"

The dress had fallen off one shoulder, and her messy strawberry blond hair framed her face in the fragile light.

"It's better than the fantasy," he whispered. "You're better than the fantasy." He traced his thumbs along the inside of her thighs. Her dress whispered out of the way, and his thumbs met in the middle, sliding slick while her eyes fluttered closed and her head tipped back.

The strap of the dress slipped farther down her arm, the fabric sliding over one breast, revealing her pert pink nipple.

"Much better," he rasped, drawing her down to take the nipple into his mouth.

He was rewarded with her gasp. She rocked forward, bracing herself with her hands in his hair, kneading his scalp while her thighs twitched under his hands.

The dress fell to her waist, and her writhing movements brought him close to the edge of control. He swiftly unfastened his pants, shoving them out of the way after retrieving a condom from his pocket.

He shifted to move on top, but she pinned down his shoulders, thighs bracing his.

"Remember," she whispered, bending to kiss him, her breasts

brushing the bare skin of his chest. "You told me how this goes when you described your fantasy."

She sat up straight, trapping his gaze with her own, lowering herself onto him, smooth and slow, until his hips bucked to meet her. His hands twisted in the quilt in a desperate attempt to keep hold of control. But there was no turning back. She was too sexy, too sweet, too passionately perfect.

He grasped her hips, holding her firm, matching her movements, and nearly dislodging them from the bed with the force of his thrusts.

She leaned forward to kiss him, and he flipped them both over, adjusting his angle and covering her with kisses, while she curled herself around him.

His brain roared for release, but he held on to paradise just as long as he could. When her cries found his ears, and her body arched high, he let the world melt around them in waves.

She was heat and sweat and scent in his arms. Her breathing was raspy, and her heart pounded hard against his own.

He smoothed back her hair, kissing her temple, then her cheek, then her hot, moist lips. He smoothed her hair again, pulling back to gaze at her exquisite face. Her eyes were closed, cheeks flushed, lips abraded in a way that made him twinge with guilt.

He wanted to say something. There had to be the perfect words for this perfect moment. But he couldn't come up with anything that didn't sound trite.

He settled on, "You're beautiful," and kissed her again.

She blinked open her eyes, her voice sleepy. "You're not so bad yourself."

"Thank you." He couldn't help but smile. "I was really hoping for 'not so bad.'"

She cocked her head, and her smile turned impish. "Do you need me to tell you you're the best I ever had?"

"Only if it's true."

"You're the best I ever had."

He searched her expression, hoping against hope that it wasn't a joke. He'd rather be the only one she'd ever had. But he knew that was ridiculous.

"I lost my virginity in college."

"So did everybody else."

"It really wasn't that great."

"It never is."

She smirked. "My point is, you didn't have much competition."

He paused, her words filling him with some unnamed emotion. "Just the one guy in college?"

She nodded.

"And it wasn't very good?" He felt a smile of pride grow on his face.

"It was terrible. Quit laughing."

"I'm not laughing."

"You're insufferable."

He hugged her close, savoring the feel of her naked body, the curl of her limbs, the softness of her breasts. "You're a treasure."

"Can you put that on my next performance evaluation?"

"Absolutely. You want me to include the rationale?"

She playfully smacked him on the arm. "I want you to approve a raise."

"You need money?" He found himself ready to step in if she did.

"I've developed expensive taste in clothes. And you just ruined a three thousand dollar dress."

He reached to where the dress was bunched at her waist and ran the filmy fabric through his fingers. "It was *so* worth it."

Ten

Jenny awoke cocooned in Mitch's arms. Sunlight was streaming through the big bedroom window, the split beam catching on the rumple of her dress discarded on an armchair beside them. A cool breeze wafted lazily down from the ceiling fan.

Mitch's body was warm where he curled around her back, one arm draped across her stomach. She shifted experimentally, stretching sore muscles.

He nuzzled her neck with a whisker-roughened face, kissing his way to the tip of her shoulder. "You okay?" he asked gently, voice morning-husky.

She shifted onto her back, taking in his sleep-crinkled eyes and beard-shadowed chin. "I'm fine." She gently touched his bare chest, concern growing as she recalled the terrible news he'd received yesterday. "You?"

"Fine," he responded, dipping to kiss her gently on the lips.

"You know what I mean," she pressed.

He slipped an arm beneath the small of her back, drawing her naked body against his own, kissing her again. "I think I'm in denial. Or maybe you're just too distracting for me to dwell on anything else." He pressed himself meaningfully against her.

"Again?" She quirked a brow, shifting one more time to test the extent of her soreness.

"Always," he muttered, his hand closing over her breast.

Her nipple instantly peaked, and desire flooded her system. Okay, so maybe she wasn't that sore.

Surprisingly, he drew back. "But you're not ready."

"I could—"

He put a finger across her lips, trailing it downward. "You've been out of practice since college."

"I was never in practice *in* college."

His grin looked decidedly possessive. "Hungry?"

She nodded, touched by his tender consideration. "Famished. And I'd kill for some coffee."

"Regular? Latte?"

"Whatever you've got."

He reached for the bedside phone. "What I've got is room service. Name your pleasure."

It was on the tip of her tongue to say him.

"Don't look at me like that," he scolded. "I'm trying to be a gentleman."

"Croissants, strawberries and regular coffee."

"You never used to play with fire," he mumbled.

"You never used to look so sexy."

He punched a button on the phone. "Tell me what's different, and I'll do it all the time."

"You're going to stay sleep-rumpled, unshaven and naked?"

"Yes," he said, staring straight at her, even though he spoke into the phone. "We'd like some croissants, some fresh strawberries and a pot of coffee."

She scooted close and whispered in his ear. "That's impractical."

His arm closed around her, and he shifted the mouthpiece to beneath his chin. "It's okay. I think they're in season." Then he spoke into the phone again. "Thank you." And he hung it up, turning back to her, grinning. "Or did you mean the naked part?"

"I meant the naked part."

"You like me naked?" he confirmed.

Jenny made a show of pulling up the sheet to peep underneath, gazing unabashedly at his sleekly muscled, magnificent body. Oh, yes. She liked him naked.

"That's it." He shifted abruptly to the edge of the bed. "I'm outta here."

She felt a jolt of unease, and pushed up on an elbow. "Did I do something wrong?"

"No." He slid his legs into last night's pants. "You're doing everything absolutely right. And if I don't leave now, I'll be all over you again."

She felt a satisfied smile grow on her face, and she let her head fall back on the pillow.

He hesitated for a split second. "You're a dangerous woman, Jenny Watson."

"Nobody's ever called me dangerous before."

"That's because they didn't see you in that dress."

She gave an exaggerated sigh. "And I guess they never will, since you tore it."

"I'll buy you a new one."

"That's silly."

"I loved you in that dress."

"You loved me out of it more," she singsonged.

He pointed through the doorway to the living room. "I'm getting the room service now, and then I'll meet you on the deck for breakfast."

Breakfast. With Mitch. After a long night of...

An unsettling thought raced into her mind, and she sat upright. She hadn't meant to ditch Jeffrey, but that had been the upshot of her behavior. "Do you think Jeffrey's mad at me?" she called out.

Mitch paused in the doorway. "I think Jeffrey's laughing at *me*."

"I don't understand."

He turned. "He all but dared me…in fact, he did dare me to dance with you."

She still didn't understand.

"He's not mad," said Mitch. "Trust me on that."

There was a knock on the suite's outer door.

"Meet me on the balcony?" Mitch repeated.

Jenny nodded, swallowing her worry. Mitch and Jeffrey were very good friends. She had to trust that Mitch knew what he was talking about.

She stayed in bed until the voices disappeared and the suite door whooshed shut. A few seconds later, she heard the balcony door slide open.

She made a quick trip to the bathroom to freshen up, then she glanced around the bedroom for something to wear. Her crumpled, stale dress seemed to be the only option. But then Mitch's tux jacket caught her eye.

She padded into the living room, slipping it on. It smelled like him, and she inhaled deeply. Then, on impulse, she looped his bow tie around her neck.

She folded the wide garment closed around her body and headed out to join him on the balcony.

When she stepped outside, he scanned her body and grinned. "You do know there are robes in the closet."

"I'm happy with this." She helped herself to a steaming cup of coffee, crossing to a padded wicker chair opposite.

A quick glance around the balcony overlooking Lady Bird Lake told her it was completely private. She sat down, leaning back, letting the jacket fall open around her.

Mitch's gaze zeroed in on her nudity, and he stared at her in silence for a long moment. "Nice tie."

She took a casual sip of the coffee. "I stole it from a guy I slept with."

"You know you're not going home today."

She spoke over the rim. "I'm not?"

He slowly shook his head. "I don't think you'll even be leaving this suite."

"I'll be late for work on Monday."

"Ever been late before?"

"Not even once."

"The boss'll forgive you."

She felt her heartbeat deepen and her stomach flutter. She swallowed. "You sure?"

His eyes turned to blue smoke. "I am positive."

They'd finally left the hotel around three o'clock in the afternoon. Mitch had bought Jenny some clothes at the hotel gift shop, and he'd assured her Jeffrey would clue in Cole and Emily. And after a walk through a lakeshore park, they'd come across a gorgeous botanical garden, wandering hand in hand amongst the trees, succulents and colorful flowers. They'd ended up in a downtown club, listening to a local country band and laughing over burgers and colas.

Then they'd spent another night together, stretching out the trip to the last second, before taking a compact private plane back to Royal.

It was nearly noon before Jenny arrived at the TCC offices. The outer door was closed, so she knew she'd beaten Mitch to work. She hustled her way along the short hallway.

"Finally," came an exasperated male voice from behind her.

Jenny glanced over her shoulder to see Brad Price catching up to her.

"Where have you been?" he demanded, taking her by surprise.

She concentrated on inserting her key into the office lock. "Good morning, Brad."

"It's afternoon," came his sharp retort.

Jenny pushed open the heavy door and glanced down at her watch. He was right about that.

Brad followed her inside. "I understood the office opened at nine?" It was more a rebuke than a question.

"I've been in Austin." Mitch's voice joined the conversation, and Jenny turned to see him stride through the open doorway. "Won an award at the Longhorn Banquet," he said to Brad. "Don't know if you heard."

"What about Jenny?" Brad challenged.

"I gave her the day off."

Brad folded his arms across the chest of his business suit. "I think we should be clear on the policy regarding office hours."

Mitch widened his stance. "Win the election in December, and you can write any policy you want."

A tense moment of silence ensued.

"I need to talk to you," said Brad.

Mitch gestured to his office. "Come on in."

Once Mitch's office door closed behind the two men, Jenny breathed a sigh of relief. She tucked away her purse, turned on her computer and pressed the button to listen to her voice mail.

As she moved into her regular routine, uncertainty crowded in. They were back on their home turf again. Would Mitch end things as abruptly as he had last time? Was she ready to have her heart crushed so quickly?

Drawing a breath, she reflexively raised her hands to her chest and pressed them down. She'd gone into this thing with her eyes wide open. She needed to guard her heart, and she needed to be ready to walk away at a moment's notice.

Mitch wasn't long-term. And the new, impulsive, carefree Jenny had to be ready to accept that. What they had at the moment was fun and exciting. She didn't need to quantify, classify and organize every nuance of their relationship.

She blew out her breath. She typed in the answer to a routine email request for information on the TCC. Then she opened a note of complaint about the proposed new clubhouse. She added it to the folder to bring to the attention of the board.

Then the phone rang, and she spent twenty minutes going over the rental options for a bride-to-be, the daughter of one of the long-term TCC members. It was going to be a spring wedding and, luckily, they were able to find a mutually workable date for the main hall and the grounds.

As she hung up the phone, Brad appeared. He bid her a reserved goodbye, and left.

"Jenny?" came Mitch's formal voice from inside his office.

Her stomach clenched with nerves. Was this going to be an abrupt and final kiss-off? Would Mitch once again suggest they forget their lovemaking ever happened and go back to normal?

"Jenny?" he called again.

She swallowed. "On my way." Then she reflexively grabbed a notepad and pen. Maybe it was nothing. Maybe he simply wanted to talk about business.

But when she paused in the doorway of the big, rectangular, dark-paneled room, he was frowning. He moved from behind the huge ebony desk, pushing the high-backed diamond leather chair out of the way.

"Close the door," he told her, and her heart sank.

She pushed back on the door, latching it shut, leaning against it for some kind of defense as he made his way past the round meeting table and the low conversation group of a leather couch and matching armchair.

"Sorry about that," he muttered.

She didn't know what to say.

"Brad's under a lot of stress right now. The election, the feud with Abigail, and now he's really under the gun with those blackmail threats."

"They're getting worse?" Jenny was one of a very small circle of people who knew Brad had received blackmail threats involving the paternity of an illegitimate child.

Mitch nodded, but he kept moving forward, closer, closer still, until he drew her into his arms. "God, I missed you."

"What about Brad?"

"Brad can find his own woman."

She cracked a smile, hugging him back as relief flooded through her.

He cradled her head against his chest.

"You dropped me off an hour ago," she reminded him. At Cole's house, she'd quickly changed into business clothes, jumped into her own car and driven directly to the office.

"Seems like longer." He cupped her face, drawing her back and leaning down to kiss her.

Relief continued to sift its way through every fiber of her body. He wasn't going to break it off, at least not this second. As the kiss went on, longing took the place of relief, until she was molded tightly against him, deepening their kiss.

He pulled back and sucked in a tight breath. "We can't do this."

For a moment, her heart stood still.

"Not in the office," he continued. Then he dropped his arms and took a step back. He raked a hand through his dark hair. "I'm thinking, at least for now, we should be circumspect while we're here."

Jenny gave herself a little shake, then nodded her head. He was saying the fling should continue, right? But they should keep it a secret? Could that work?

Certainly Emily and Cole had figured it out, since she was supposed to have stayed at Cole's rented house in Austin. And Jeffrey knew they'd left the banquet together. How clandestine was Mitch thinking they could be?

She longed to ask him what he meant, but with the relationship so new and tentative, she didn't dare go into specific detail. Besides, that was old Jenny. New Jenny could go with the flow.

Maybe.

"I'm going to try to focus on work," Mitch told her with a sheepish grin. "Can you do the same? For a few hours? Then I'll drop by Cole's later?"

Jenny nodded more vigorously this time. She could do that.

"It's a weird time," he said, suddenly sounding tired, face

pinched in worry. He shook his head, one hand going out to brace against the back of an armchair. "You helped me over the past two days. I'm grateful. But it's starting to sink in, you know?"

She knew. She remembered. Their exhilarating weekend together was one thing. But his career had also ended. She took a step toward him. "Anything I can do?"

"I wish there was." Unexpectedly, a small smile twitched the corners of his mouth. "There is one thing you can do. But your special brand of physical and emotional therapy will have to wait until after business hours."

She was relieved to see the worry ease from his expression. "You know I'm just a temporary stopgap."

"I'll take it anyway." His midnight blue gaze bore into hers.

"Did you think about this possibility at all?" she found herself asking.

"I tried very hard not to."

"You had no kind of a plan?"

He shook his head. "Every single one of my coaches taught me to visualize success, not failure. When the tackles are bearing down on you, and the receiver is out of position, you don't dare, not even for one second, picture that ball missing the hands of the receiver. It's the kiss of death."

She found herself easing closer still.

"So, yeah, I knew this might be a career-ending injury," he admitted. "But I never let my mind go down the pathway to what that meant. I'm running blind here, Jenny."

She longed to reach out to him. But she mustered her self-control. "Can I hug you later?" she asked, voice low and throbbing.

"Hugging is the least of what I was counting on for later."

Jenny was surprised to find Emily sitting at the breakfast bar in Cole's kitchen, munching her way through one of his cook's famous oatmeal almond cookies.

"You just get home?" asked Emily.

"Are you waiting for me?" Jenny slowed to a halt, wondering how much, if anything, Emily had figured out.

Emily glanced a little guiltily toward the back hallway. "I'm visiting Cole."

Well, well, well. This was interesting.

Jenny pulled out one of the breakfast bar stools and climbed up, cornerwise to Emily. She searched her friend's expression for a clue. "*You're* visiting Cole?"

Emily responded with a sly grin, taking a slow bite of her cookie and chewing. "*You* stayed an extra day in Austin."

Jenny returned the smile self-consciously. "I did."

"We couldn't help but notice you didn't come back to the rental house."

"Any more of those cookies left?" asked Jenny, leaning forward and reaching for the brightly colored tin. She eased off the lid and plunged her hand inside, concentrating on selecting one of the round, grainy treats. Then she glanced around the kitchen to confirm they were alone. "Mitch had a nice hotel suite."

"And, so…?" Emily probed.

Jenny shrugged. "So, I saw the hotel suite. Liked it. Decided to stay awhile."

"And?" Emily leaned forward. "Give. He's with you now? What changed his mind?"

Jenny hadn't wanted to examine that question too closely. Her best guess was that Mitch had changed his mind about her being too fragile to risk dating.

"Jenny?" Emily prompted.

"I don't know what to think," Jenny confided. "I guess I'm just taking it one day at a time, you know?"

Emily nodded, reaching out to pat Jenny's hand. "I hear you. Cole and I are just testing the waters. Messing around to see if anything happens."

Jenny took another contemplative bite of the cookie. "Messing around? Literally?"

"Started off a bit rocky at the dance," Emily told her in a low tone.

"Yeah?"

"I asked him if he thought Emilio would be willing to get me pregnant."

Jenny nearly choked on an almond. "You *what?*"

"After some discussion," Emily continued matter-of-factly, "we decided Cole should do the job himself."

"Seriously?"

Emily nodded.

"That must have been some dance."

"Yeah. Well." Emily got a faraway look in her eyes. "Apparently, you don't have to be that tall to be a kicker. I figure my sons can try out for the special teams."

"Or shortstop." Cole appeared from the hallway, crossed the kitchen and helped himself to a cookie from the tin, taking a position beside the patio door and leaning against the wall. "They might want to play baseball."

Jenny glanced from one to the other. They had to be joking. Didn't they? "Are you two seriously thinking about making a baby?"

"Don't misunderstand," Cole continued. "I plan to ask her to marry me just as soon as I find the right rock. But right now I'm kinda busy keeping her in my bed and away from the offensive line."

Again, Emily nodded her agreement.

"Ain't that a bitch?" Mitch's voice joined the conversation.

"Hey, Mitch," Cole greeted amicably, while Mitch took in the cookie fest and apparently decided to join them, helping himself.

"Have a good time in Austin?" asked Cole.

Mitch grinned, settling in next to Jenny. "Had a great time. You?" He bit down on half of the cookie.

"The best," said Cole.

Jenny took in the glow on Emily's and Cole's faces, and found her emotions calming down. They might be joking about getting pregnant, but their true message was that they'd fallen in love.

"You're getting married?" she asked, wanting to confirm the meaning of Cole's offhand remark.

Emily made a show of a heavy sigh. "I guess I will have to marry the guy."

Cole pulled her close against him. "She finally came to her senses."

"He's not that short," she admitted. "And he does have this incredible—"

Cole cut her off with a solid kiss, and Jenny found her gaze straying to Mitch. His answering smile warmed her heart.

"I brought you a present," he whispered, straightening away from Emily and Cole.

Curious, Jenny twisted to watch him cross the kitchen floor. He retrieved a flat gold box from the telephone table just inside the kitchen doorway.

"What is it?" she automatically asked, thoroughly puzzled by the gesture.

"Open it and see." He set it on the island countertop in front of her.

"Is this a joke?" For some reason, she steeled herself. What was this all about?

"I'm dead serious." He pushed it in her direction.

"Should we leave you two alone?" Cole asked.

Mitch gave him a mocking eye-roll. "It's not X-rated."

"Too bad," said Emily, and everyone looked her way. She shrugged. "It could be fun."

"Open it up," Mitch prompted Jenny.

She took a bracing breath and lifted the lid.

Pulling back the mauve tissue paper, she found a gently folded rainbow silk dress. It took her a moment to realize what he'd done, and then another long moment to speak. "You bought a new one?"

"It was a great dress," said Mitch, moving up close behind her, gazing over her shoulder and smoothing his broad palm down her hair to the back of her neck.

"What happened to the last one?" asked Cole, a thread of laughter in his voice.

"You'll never find out," Mitch answered.

Emily reached out and touched Jenny's arm. "You looked fabulous in it."

Jenny didn't know what to say. It was an expensive gift, a very thoughtful gift. She did love the dress, but things like this were going to make it hard for her to keep her relationship with Mitch in perspective.

"Would you have preferred something different?" he asked her in a low voice.

She shook her head. She would have preferred to not feel this tightness in her chest, this rush of soft emotions and the urge to bury herself against him and hold on forever. She felt vulnerable and frightened. The old Jenny would have demanded to know what the gift meant, and where Mitch thought he was going with all this.

But she couldn't do that. And, unfortunately, the new Jenny didn't have a coping mechanism for a guy who was sending out mixed messages.

"Anyone up for dinner?" asked Cole, breaking the silence. "Seafood? Gillian's Landing?"

"Sounds great to me," said Emily, sliding off her high chair.

Cole braced her while she settled her feet on the floor.

"Okay by you?" Mitch asked Jenny. "We can go back to my place and grill something instead."

Jenny shook her head. "No. Gillian's sounds great." Better not to spend too much time alone with Mitch, dreaming of things that might never be.

* * *

Later that night, Mitch reflected on how much he loved being alone with Jenny.

He lay in his bed, propped up on one elbow, the light sheet covering him from the waist down.

Jenny had slipped into one of his faded football jerseys and rolled the long sleeves up to her elbows. It was green and white, with the number twenty-two across the back, and it hung nearly down to her knees.

Her hair was mussed from their lovemaking, and she couldn't have looked more adorable.

"And this one?" she asked, lifting a gold trophy from the shelf beside his dresser.

"High school," he told her. "Junior year."

She held the etched plaque close to her face, squinting. "Player of The Year. All State."

"It was a good year. I had a lot of lucky breaks." He patted the bed beside him. "You must be getting cold out there."

She replaced the trophy, picking up the next one. "You need to dust these."

"If you're going through the entire set, it's going to take all night," he complained.

"The Dallas Devils?"

"College."

"It's heavy." She hefted the tall trophy.

"Careful."

"I won't break it."

Mitch rolled out of bed. "I don't want it to break you."

She giggled, as if his worry was absurd.

He strode across the hardwood floor and lifted the trophy from her hands, setting it safely back on the shelf.

"What are these?" She opened a cherrywood box that his mother had given him when he was about fifteen.

"Come back to bed."

"They're rings," she exclaimed, running her finger through the box. "They're gorgeous. Look at these."

"I've seen them."

"The Lightning Bowl. The Ibex Cup."

He bent to kiss her tender neck. "You can look at those any old time."

"Are these real diamonds?"

"I don't know. Probably."

"How many of these have you won?" She checked through the contents of the box.

"I have no idea." His kisses were making their way toward her lips.

She held a ring up to the light. "Tell me that's not a real emerald."

He didn't bother looking. "That's not a real emerald."

"You're lying. Look at that color and clarity."

"You want the ring? Take the ring."

"I don't think it'll fit." She dropped it and let it fall loosely onto the base of her thumb, spinning it around for a moment before putting it back.

Mitch gave up on kissing, pawing his way through the box and extracting a gold ring with a flat face, a ruby chip and the entwined platinum letters *S* and *C* in relief. "Try this one."

She accepted it in her palm. "It's nice."

"My first." He smiled. "Sixth grade. It might fit." He snagged her hand, slipping it on to the ring finger of her right hand.

Laughing, she tried to pull away.

But he held her still. "See, it fits fine."

"I'm not taking your ring."

"Why not?" Grinning, he kissed her palm. "It's not like I'm going to use it again. You want to go steady?" The words were out of his mouth before he could stop them.

Her smile disappeared. "Don't do that."

"I was just—"

"I know how you feel, Mitch. Don't mess around." She determinedly tugged off the ring.

He opened his mouth to explain. But what could he say? He'd done nothing but make his position on a serious relationship repeatedly and abundantly clear to her for the past few weeks.

"Sorry," he mumbled.

She dropped the ring back into the box. "Nothing to be sorry for." Then she pasted a determined smile on her face, snapped the wooden box shut and set it back on the shelf. "You've had an amazing career," she bravely carried on, but there was a warmth missing from the tone of her voice.

"You're what's amazing," he told her honestly, but she shifted away.

He wanted to kick himself. He'd hurt her feelings again. Hurt her feelings, frightened her and forced a cool distance between them, when all he wanted to do was carry her back to his bed and make love to her, or maybe just hold her in his arms for the next few hours, or days or weeks.

Eleven

After Mitch's stupid slipup about going steady last night, Jenny had left his house. It had been nothing but a joke, but it had obviously rattled her. And now he didn't know how to fix it.

This morning, he was frustrated and in no mood for Cole's interference. He glared at Cole across his office desk. But Cole didn't back down, parroting Mitch's words. "No, this is absolutely *not* rich, successful Cole Maddison, throwing *poor, pathetic* Mitch Hayward a bone."

"Then give me an explanation."

"The explanation is that you should get your head out of your ass."

"You're saying the White House randomly thought of me? A washed-up quarterback from Royal, Texas, who hasn't won a significant sports award in nearly a decade?"

"No. Someone at the White House probably watched your touchdown rush in the Folder Cup, saw your charitable endorsements to Childhood Special Teams, read about your work with underprivileged teenage players, noticed the hundreds of thousands of hits on your fan site and heard about your *Youth Outreach Award from the governor last week!*"

"Keep your voice down." Mitch's office door was closed, but Jenny could arrive at any moment.

"Then listen to me. This is not some fabricated, make-work, patronage position invented out of pity. You'd have a staff, a budget, three regional offices and a mandate that covers the country."

Mitch drew back, trying to wrap his head around the unexpected proposal. "And it's the *President's* council."

"The President's Council on Physical Fitness." Cole's voice was flat, his frustration still evident. "You'd be the Director for Children and Youth."

Mitch tried to picture it, but couldn't.

"Listen," said Cole, backing off and plunking down in one of the two guest chairs at the front of Mitch's desk. "It sucks that you got hurt. It truly does. But you did, and you can't change that. So, you can sit around and cry about it, or you can pick yourself up and dust yourself off, and get going on the rest of your life."

Mitch resented Cole's implication. "Have I, *ever once,* come whining to you in self-pity?"

"You've got a lot of self-discipline. I'll give you that. But actions speak louder than words." Cole glanced around the big office. "In December, this gig's going to end. And then what?"

Mitch had been trying hard not to think about that. But Cole was dead right on that count.

"And it has to be in D.C.?" Mitch forced himself to think through the potential of the unexpected offer.

"You gotta be where the action is. Part of your job will be to schmooze senators and congressmen to make sure the program is well funded."

"I don't schmooze."

Cole barked out a laugh. "After the embezzlement and sabotage here two years ago, you nearly single-handedly brought the TCC back from the brink of disaster to a solid, thriving organization."

Mitch gave a snort of disbelief. "If this paternity thing with Brad blows up…"

"I'm sure you'll deal with that, too. My point is, you do know how to schmooze. You've got the gift for talking anybody into anything."

Mitch knew he could hold his own when it came to persuasion. He'd never thought of it as lobbying, but he supposed that wasn't too much of a stretch.

"And your celebrity doesn't hurt one little bit," Cole continued. "Plus, you've proven your ability to engage young people beyond the realm of sports. I can't imagine anyone more perfect for the job."

"Do you need a soapbox of some kind to stand on?"

"Was that a joke about my height?"

Mitch barked out a laugh at Cole's unexpected response. "Emily really got to you over the short thing, didn't she?"

"Emily…has seen the light."

"Congratulations on that, by the way."

Cole gave a nod of acceptance. Then he waggled his brow. "Take a look." He reached into his jacket pocket and extracted a black velvet box, handing it over to Mitch.

"You're going to ask her?"

"I am."

Mitch snapped open the box to reveal a big square-cut diamond surrounded by miniature sapphires. Something hitched in his stomach, and he found himself thinking about the ring he'd offered Jenny last night. Stupid.

He had nothing in him but a joke, while Cole was ready to take a lifetime plunge.

"You worried?" he asked, genuinely curious about how Cole could be so certain about his decision.

"Not really. I'm sure she'll say yes."

That wasn't what Mitch meant. But he had to admire Cole's confidence. "As long as you're sure."

"What's not to be sure about?"

"It's for the rest of your life."

"Hey, when you know, you know."

Mitch closed the box and handed it back. Would he know? Should he know? Did he know?

"Did you like the ring?" Cole asked.

"It's fine," Mitch answered absently.

Cole grinned. "You couldn't give a damn, could you?"

"Not in my frame of reference," he lied, pretending he wasn't thinking about putting more than just a football ring on Jenny's finger.

He shook away the ridiculous idea. This was a brand-new infatuation, a knee-jerk reaction to his career ending. And if he tried to make more of it, tried to force it, he risked hurting Jenny even more than he already had.

"D.C., you say?" he asked Cole.

"Yeah. Why do you keep asking?"

When he thought about leaving, Mitch's thoughts went straight to Jenny.

There was no good choice in all this.

"Go to D.C.," Cole insisted. "Check it out. See if it fits. If it does, you'll have a great Beltway office. You'll be doing good for the youth of America. It'll keep you out of trouble. And they'll pay mileage on your jet."

Mitch drummed his fingers on the desktop. He supposed there was no harm in talking. And, who knew, maybe they'd be willing to wait a few weeks, or maybe a couple of months. Surely by then his relationship with Jenny would have run its course. She'd probably be itching to be rid of him.

"You'll keep this to yourself?" he asked Cole.

"Won't tell a soul. Not even Emily."

Especially not Emily. If Mitch did this, *if* he did this, he'd have to be very careful about when and how he told Jenny in order to keep from hurting her.

As she stared at the three sets of house plans taped to the wall in the mostly bare, airy room on the second floor of Cole's house, Jenny tried to forget about the debacle two days ago, when Mitch had offered her the ring.

Mitch's joke about going steady had driven home for her just how quickly and how thoroughly she'd fallen under his spell. In the split second it had taken for her to come to her senses, she'd realized how desperately she wanted go steady with him, to have him be an ongoing part of her life.

"Time's up," Emily said from beside her. "They're shaping the foundation tomorrow. Are you going with your heart or your head?"

Emily had been the one to insist that they continue to consider all three sets of plans.

Jenny's heart was leading her toward the whimsical French country house. But she'd trusted her heart last night, and look where it got her.

What started off as a relaxed romantic interlude had ended in awkwardness and embarrassment. She'd all but fled from Mitch's house, and then this morning, he'd abruptly left town with the lamest of excuses, some vague story about paperwork and the football team.

"I'm going with my head." She moved to stand in front of the two-story, three-bedroom, telling herself she'd be happy there.

Emily came up beside her. "Funny. Lately, I'm leaning toward my heart."

Jenny forced herself to smile, not wanting to inflict her mood on Emily's happiness. "Did he ask you yet?"

"Tonight."

"He gave you advance warning?"

"He says he found the right ring. And we have reservations on the rooftop at Chez Jacques. I can fill in the blanks."

"You're going all the way to Houston for dinner?"

Emily waved a dismissive hand. "There's a helicopter involved. Millionaires are crazy."

Jenny leaned into Emily's shoulder, determined to be happy for her good friend. "That's fantastic."

"It is," Emily sighed. "You can't even imagine how smart he is. He gets calls from New York and D.C., Switzerland and Brazil, movers and shakers in the high-tech world, politicians, even movie stars. They want his advice. They want to be his friend. And he's funny, wickedly funny. But he's not geeky. He's not even short."

Jenny couldn't help but smile at that. "He magically stopped being short? Imagine that."

Emily gave her hair a little toss. "Five-eleven's not short. I was giving him grief about it on the dance floor, when I was asking about Emilio." A blush formed on her face. "Man, was Cole ticked off about that. Anyway, he's making a point, and I realized he was towering over me. And then I realized how much sense he was making, and how much I respected his opinion."

She rolled her eyes. "Listen to me. I sound like a dork. Back to your house."

"You're not a dork."

Emily pointed. "So, this one."

"This one." Jenny nodded. "Definitely."

"I would have bet you were going to go the other way." Emily cocked her head at the French country house. "I was beginning to think—"

"Mitch left this morning," Jenny blurted out.

Emily drew back in obvious surprise. "Huh?"

"Not that I didn't expect it. It was bound to happen sooner or later." Jenny had given away her insecurities two nights ago, probably panicked Mitch. Why couldn't she have just joked right back? Why did she have to freeze up like a schoolgirl?

"What do you mean, he left?"

"He went to D.C."

"On business?"

"He said it was football business."

Emily searched Jenny's expression. "And?"

"And, I think he lied." Suddenly dizzy, Jenny braced a hand against the wall.

Emily reached for her. "Jenny?"

"I'm fine."

Emily took her arm and helped her to one of two armchairs in the corner of the large rectangular room.

"What the hell is going on?"

Embarrassed, Jenny eased down into the chair. "Same old, same old. I'm crazy about him, and he's just having a good time. I thought I could handle it. I really did."

"Did he say that?"

Jenny shook her head. "Two nights ago…well, he joked, and I kind of freaked, and this morning he left. And I don't know what that means. And I'm trying not to care. But I do care." Her chest hitched. "I really do."

Emily crouched down next to the armchair, placing her hand over Jenny's. "I'm so sorry I went on about me and Cole."

"I'm sorry to be such a wet blanket." Jenny felt a sting in the back of her eyes. "Honestly, I don't know why I'm so emotional."

"PMS?"

Jenny laughed. Wouldn't it be nice to have such a simple explanation? In fact, now that she thought about it, maybe that was the explanation. She did the math in her head.

She usually got her period on a Saturday. Was it this Saturday? It had been nearly three weeks since the wedding, and before that—

Her stomach crashed into a free fall.

"Jenny? You just turned white as a sheet." Emily tightened her hold.

Jenny struggled not to panic. "Do you have a calendar?"

"Sure. In my phone." Emily produced the phone and pressed a few buttons with her thumb, holding it out for Jenny to see.

"Which weekend did we go to the Albatross Club?"

Emily turned the phone so that she could see the calendar. "That had to be the twelfth. Because it was a pay week for me."

A roar sounded in Jenny's ears. "Oh, no."

"Oh, no, what?"

"Oh, frickin' *no.*"

"What?"

"I had my period that weekend."

"And?"

"And, I'm just doing the math."

"But—" Emily's eyes went wide, and her mouth formed a perfect circle.

Jenny stood up from the armchair and took two staggering steps backward. "It can't be. No, no, no."

"The night of the wedding?"

Jenny made an inarticulate exclamation.

"You must have used a condom."

"We did. We *did.*"

"Then the mathematical odds are in your favor."

"Right."

Emily was right. Jenny forced herself to calm down. What she needed now was more information.

At the interview in D.C., Mitch had been offered everything Cole predicted and more. It was a significant and meaningful job, with a laundry list of perks and a chance to work with kids all over the nation. If he had to leave professional football, there was no better way to do it than this.

So why was he hesitating?

Why had he asked the White House Senior Advisor for a few days to make up his mind? It wasn't geography. He'd never planned to stay in Royal long-term. And if he wasn't with the team, it didn't matter where he lived. The salary was great, plus he'd built up an almost embarrassing nest egg through appearances and endorsements over the years.

So, it wasn't the money. It was Jenny. It always came back to Jenny. He didn't want to leave her.

He paused in the lobby of the Rathcliffe Hotel, gazing unseeingly through a shop window. First he only saw a reflection of the lights behind him, then slowly his eyes focused on the shiny jewels in the display. Against a backdrop of autumn maple leaves, gold necklaces, platinum bracelets and colored stones of every description were arranged on crystal stands.

He found himself staring at a round diamond solitaire, set in platinum, with tiny emeralds at each side.

"Nobody buys an engagement ring in a hotel gift shop," came a familiar voice.

Mitch shook himself back to life and turned to see Jeffrey. "What are you doing here?"

"We're playing in Baltimore tomorrow night."

"And that brings you to this hotel how?" Mitch resented Jeffrey's sudden appearance. He really wanted to be alone.

"Cole told me you'd be here."

Mitch cursed out loud. "He *swore* he'd keep quiet about the job."

"He didn't tell me *why* you were here. Though you just did. What job?"

"It's nothing."

"You're looking at a job in D.C.?"

"None of your business."

"What about Jenny?"

"*None* of your business."

Jeffrey braced a hand against the wall. "You're zoned out staring at engagement rings here, Mitch."

"I'm not staring at anything. I'm just zoned out." Mitch paused. "I'm thinking about the job."

"So, that's it. You just leave her? Thanks for the memories."

"It was always going to be like that." Just not yet. *Not yet.*

"You're a moron, you know that?"

Mitch clamped his jaw against an angry outburst. What the hell was Jeffrey doing here anyway? "Why are you here?"

Jeffrey's tone abruptly changed. "I heard the verdict came in on your shoulder."

"Twenty to life," said Mitch, knowing he sounded bitter.

"Man, I'm sure sorry about that."

Jeffrey and Mitch's friendship definitely didn't lend itself to talking about their feelings.

"Don't worry about it."

"It sucks."

"I'll live."

"Mitch." There was clear compassion in Jeffrey's tone. He was in a better position than most people to understand what Mitch was going through.

"You know," Mitch gave in. "Half the time, I think, yeah, I've had a good run, better than most, longer than most. I am thirty, and it ain't gonna last forever. Other times, I want to put my fist through a wall."

"Might want to use the left."

Mitch coughed out a cold laugh. "Good advice."

Jeffrey slid his glance away. "You know I'm here for you, right?"

"Thanks." They didn't need to belabor the point. But Mitch appreciated the offer.

Jeffrey cleared his throat. "So, when does the job start?"

"I haven't said yes."

"Are you going to say yes?"

Good question. Mitch shrugged. "I guess it's more about the timing." So, how long did he need? Two weeks? Two months? The TCC Board had made it clear all along they would understand and make arrangements if he needed to make a career change. But how could he possibly pick an end date for the relationship?

"And more about Jenny?" Jeffrey guessed.

"It's complicated," Mitch allowed, tired of pussyfooting around.

"Make it simple."

"I can't."

"You know, man. If you don't want her."

Mitch felt his blood pressure spike, and his hands curled into fists. He struggled not to snarl at Jeffrey. "You can't have her."

"Dude. Did you just see what you did there?"

"Showed some good taste?"

"Your head flies off at the mere thought that some other guy might look at her."

"Not every other guy." Just guys like Jeffrey who would most certainly hurt her. Mostly. And, yeah, okay, all the other guys, too.

"Yes," Jeffrey articulated slowly. "Every other guy. And I've already made my position crystal clear when it comes to Jenny. So you have less reason to worry about me than most guys. But look at you."

Mitch couldn't argue. For a long moment, he found himself imagining her expression if he was to give her that ring in the window. And then what? Marry her?

Part of him wanted to go for it, but a more rational part worried this was all happening too fast. It couldn't be real.

"Let's go grab a beer," Jeffrey suggested.

"Only if we change the subject."

"No problem."

"The lounge is on five."

"Let's leave the hotel. There are some great places down Pennsylvania Ave."

Mitch shrugged. What did it matter? Liquor was probably as good a way as any to switch up his thought patterns. And he didn't really care where he drank it.

A uniformed doorman let them out, and they turned right, going against the majority of pedestrian traffic along the wide sidewalk. It was four in the afternoon, late enough that the business crowd was swelling the streets, while last-minute shoppers rushed through their errands. The street was a maze of cars, minivans, buses and high-end automobiles ferrying VIPs from meetings to dinners to corporate and political functions.

"See, if it was me," said Jeffrey, pulling on a glass shop door. "I'd wow her with something along these lines."

Confused, Mitch glanced at the sign. Too late, he realized Jeffrey had just ushered him into the showroom at Tiffany's.

"Very funny." Mitch gave a mock laugh, while a salesman quickly approached them, obviously appraising the quality of their suits and watches as he did.

"Good afternoon, sir," the man greeted heartily.

"Just looking," Mitch quickly put in.

"Something in a solitaire," said Jeffrey. "The last one he liked had a couple of small emeralds."

The man beamed. "I'm Roger Stromberg. At your service. Please, let me show you our Esteme collection."

He motioned them toward one side of the store, and Jeffrey immediately fell in behind.

"I'm outta here," Mitch declared.

Jeffrey clapped a firm hand on his back. "Wouldn't try it if I was you. You've got a bum shoulder, and I'm a better tackle."

"This joke's gone on long enough."

"He's got cold feet," Jeffrey loudly explained to the salesman, dropping his large frame into one of two padded chairs in front of a display case.

"I understand." The suited salesman gave a sage nod. "Thing to remember in this circumstance is that picking out a ring doesn't commit you to anything. We're happy to keep it on hold for a period of time. Or we'll simply use today to make sure you understand your options. Then if, at a later date, you want to make a quick decision, you're all set.

"These ones here—" he pulled three rings from the display and set them in their cases on top of the glass "—are all flaw-less, D and E." He glanced up. "Do you mind if I ask your price range?"

"Not an object," said Jeffrey.

Mitch gave up and took a seat. "I sure hope you're the guy popping the question," he said to Jeffrey. "Because I'm just a spectator on this."

Jeffrey and the salesman exchanged a significant glance, but Mitch just chuckled to himself. Jeffrey wasn't going to goad him into anything so rash as choosing a ring.

Twelve

Jenny was going to be a single mother.

She couldn't believe it. She could barely bring herself to acknowledge it, never mind say it out loud. She'd checked the test wand four times this morning. Twice in the bathroom, again halfway down the stairs, then she'd pulled it out of the trash once, just to be sure.

The line was blue.

She was pregnant.

Thank goodness Mitch was out of town. She'd landed right smack-dab in her mother's predicament. Difference was, she wasn't going to repeat her mother's mistake.

She absolutely would not let a man marry her because she was pregnant and then start hating her. Still, in her weaker moments, she'd caught herself thinking about telling Mitch, imagined him breaking into a wide smile, telling her he was happy, assuring her they were going to make it work. But then she'd exit Wonderland and pull herself together.

Reality was hitting her fast and hard. Since arriving at the office, she'd twice had to dash to the bathroom to vomit. And she was facing the stark fact that she was going to have a baby all by herself.

Just like her mother, she'd have to hold down a job, juggle day care and PTA meetings, make budgetary ends meet and try to comfort a lonely little boy or girl who desperately wanted siblings.

Working her way compulsively around the office, she shoved the sparkling clean coffeepot back into the freshly polished machine that sat on a compact, shiny countertop in the corner of the office. Then she centered the wicker basket of assorted teas that she'd lined up alphabetically by variety: blueberry, chamomile, Earl Grey, ginger, Irish breakfast, jasmine green, lemon, mint. They had only one peppermint left, and all the other packets were in even numbers. She briefly considered brewing and drinking it, but her stomach had rebelled.

Again, she said a silent thanks that Mitch was in D.C. If he'd been in the office, today would have been an even bigger disaster.

She rewiped the shelf that held the sugar packets, checked the coffee can to make sure it was at least half-full, centered the stainless steel faucet above the sink and refolded the dishcloth.

The desk phone rang, but she ignored it.

The last three numbers on the readout had been Emily's. Jenny had purposely escaped from the house this morning before Emily and Cole saw her. She knew if she didn't answer the office phone, Emily would show up at lunchtime. But she'd face that in an hour.

She glanced at the clock on the wall, noting it read 11:02. She automatically checked her watch, making sure the times synced up. Then she crossed to her desk and sat down, folding her hands on the pristine wooden top, trying to figure out what on earth to do next.

The red message light was flashing on the face of the phone. She didn't want to listen to Emily's voice and feel the guilt that came with ignoring her best friend. But there was an off chance it was a TCC member who needed something. And she couldn't ignore what might be an important matter. There were three weddings coming up this month.

Her throat closed up, and she was forced to swallow the lump. Three radiant, blissful brides would say their vows under the Leadership, Justice and Peace plaque, something that would never happen for Jenny. True love was obviously not in the cards for her. Fate had single motherhood in mind instead.

Blinking the moisture from her eyes, she determinedly lifted the telephone handset, pressing the button for voice mail. She entered the password and heard the computer-generated voice inform her there were two new messages.

The first one was from Emily, short and to the point, obviously worried and telling her to call back just as soon as possible. The second was from a member. Thankfully, it was for general information, and it could wait a few hours. Then she punched in Mitch's number and his pass-code, learning there was another message on his account.

She tapped her pen on the pad of message paper as a hearty male voice spoke. "It was great to get your message yesterday," it said. "I know you didn't ask me to call, but I didn't want to waste any time in offering my thanks and my congratulations. The entire D.C. office is looking forward to working with you, Mitch. As I said in the interview, we're flexible on timing. But I will courier over the employment documents in the next few days. As I'm sure you can appreciate, working this close to the White House staff, there's a fairly rigorous security procedure, and we should get that started. Call me when you get back to Royal. If I'm not in the office, Melanie will give you my private line. It was really great to meet you. We'll talk soon."

There was a click, and the line went silent. Jenny sat frozen, the phone still at her ear while the computerized voice listed the voice mail options.

"End of new messages," the computer voice said.

Jenny couldn't believe it. Mitch had gone to a job interview? He'd rushed out of town yesterday to find himself a new job?

She gave a slightly hysterical laugh. So much for going steady. He was obviously leaving Royal. And he was definitely leaving her.

Any small, lingering hope that she might have had for their future evaporated in the blink of an eye.

"Press star to disconnect," instructed the computerized voice.

Jenny's stomach rolled. Her gaze flew back to the clock on the wall. Mitch was probably on his way home right now. If he didn't make it to the office this afternoon, he'd definitely be here tomorrow morning.

What was she going to do? How was she going to face him? How could she possibly even hope to pretend everything was normal?

What if she had morning sickness tomorrow? Worse, what if she was sick every morning for the rest of the week, or the rest of the month? She'd never keep the pregnancy a secret.

She came shakily to her feet just as Emily burst through the door.

"Why aren't you answering?" Emily demanded, swinging the door shut and barreling forward. Then she halted midstride.

"Oh, no." Her hands reached out, and she came forward again, rounding the desk and pulling Jenny firmly into her arms. "You are, aren't you?"

Jenny nodded, twin tears leaking out. "The test this morning was positive."

"Oh, honey." Emily smoothed her hands down Jenny's back. "Why did you leave without me? Never mind. It doesn't matter. It's going to be okay. I promise you, it's going to be okay."

But it wasn't going to be okay. It was going to be very, very far from okay for a very long time.

"I have to get out of here," said Jenny, her voice shaking.

"Of course you do." Emily drew back to look at her. "We'll go to Cole's house. Or are you hungry? Should we go to the diner?"

Jenny's stomach lurched at the thought of greasy fries and heavy milkshakes.

"Uh-oh," Emily repeated. "Is it bad?"

"Pretty bad. But, oh." Jenny closed her eyes and waited for the nausea to pass. "I really have to get out of here. Not just out of the office. Out of Royal altogether. I have to leave before Mitch gets back."

Emily nodded. "You're worried about how to tell him. I understand."

"I'm not *telling* him at all."

"Well, no," Emily said gently. "It doesn't even have to be today."

Jenny grasped her friend's upper arms. "Emily. Listen to me. Mitch told me a thousand different ways that he wasn't in this for the long haul. He's nowhere near ready to commit. He went to D.C. for a job interview. And he accepted a position. He's leaving Royal. He's leaving me."

"But—"

"But, nothing. He doesn't want me. He sure doesn't want a baby. And I am not   I am *not* going to have my child raised by an unwilling father."

Emily's eyes narrowed in confusion. "You can't keep it a secret. He has friends in Royal. Cole will—"

"Not forever," Jenny conceded, knowing she'd have to eventually tell Mitch he was a father. "But I can keep it a secret for now." At least, she could if she wasn't around him. If she could figure out how to get away, a plausible excuse to get out of Royal until Mitch left permanently for D.C.

She braced her hand on the edge of the desk. "I need a plan. A good excuse to leave. Then he'll come back, resign from TCC, leave for his new job in D.C., and then I'll decide what to do and when to do it."

Emily bit her bottom lip. "I don't know, Jenny."

"It's the only way." Her throat closed over again, and her voice broke. "I can't trap him. I *won't* trap him, Em."

Emily wrapped a firm arm around Jenny's shoulders. "Then I'll help you. Of course I'll help you. You can go up to the cottage at Lake Angel, for a week, or two, or three. As long as you need. Tell Mitch it was an emergency. Leave him a message."

Jenny was nodding. "I could do that. I could tell him someone is sick." Her hand went to her stomach. "I'm definitely sick. And I can say I'm at a friend's house. I'll be at yours. It's not even a lie."

Emily gave a sad smile. "It's not even a lie."

Jenny sniffed, sitting down. "Are you sure your folks won't mind?"

"Not a bit. They won't be at the lake for months. The cottage is the perfect place for you to regroup."

Jenny turned her chair and started to type. She could barely make her fingers form the words that would take her away from Mitch forever. She was suddenly bone tired. She wanted to crawl into bed and sleep for a month. She didn't want to face Mitch or anyone else.

As Mitch powered his Corvette away from the small airport on the outskirts of Royal, his hand strayed from the gearshift to pat the small square package tucked away in his suit jacket pocket, while his mind settled comfortably into thoughts of Jenny. If someone had told him forty-eight hours ago that he'd be buying an engagement ring, he'd have told them they were out of their mind.

But things changed, people learned. They learned things about themselves, and they figured out things about others that had been staring them in the face for months. What Mitch had learned was that he wanted Jenny, now and forever. He loved her. And he wasn't about to let one more day go by without telling her so.

He swung off the interstate and took the three corners to River Road. He'd driven this route a thousand times, knew every curve, every bump, every blind spot. But he'd never driven it faster, never wished it were shorter. And by the time he pulled into the TCC parking lot, he was having a very stern talk with himself to calm down and curb his enthusiasm.

He couldn't tell Jenny he loved her next to the coffeemaker. And he sure couldn't propose to her at the office. He pushed the shifter into First, set the park brake and turned off the key.

He had to take her out on a date tonight, somewhere exotic and wildly romantic. Maybe they'd go to the beach again. There had to be dozens of fine restaurants overlooking Galveston Bay. He wanted something with candlelight and white linen, a private little alcove where he could say all the things he needed to say.

He took the TCC stairs two at a time, striding through the front foyer, heading directly to the second floor, down the short hallway and into the outer office.

"Jenny?" he breathed, before he realized she wasn't there.

He quickly moved to his own office, entering through the open door, expecting to see her inside, straightening his papers, watering his plants, putting his mail into those neat little piles, like she did every day.

He drew another blank and frowned.

Maybe she was in the conference room, or the ladies' room. He told himself to wait it out, but his feet took him back across the outer office, down the hallway and into the conference room.

It was empty, and he couldn't very well check the ladies' room. So he headed back to the office, cooling his heels, gazing unseeingly at the familiar surroundings.

It was quiet, somehow too quiet. It felt like a weekend, and it took him a moment to realize it was because her computer was shut off. Her chair was neatly pushed into the desk. There wasn't a single paper on her desktop, and the morning's mail was piled haphazardly in her in-basket.

Was Jenny away?

Could she have missed a day's work?

He ventured closer to her desk, spying a crisp white envelope in the center of the desk. His name was scrawled across it in Jenny's handwriting.

Mitch picked it up, staring, getting an unsettled feeling in the pit of his stomach. She'd left him a note? Why didn't she email, or text, or give him a call if she had to miss work?

He tore off the end of the envelope and slid out a single piece of paper.

Dear Mitch, it opened.

He read further through the letter, becoming more confused by the second. Jenny was gone?

He flipped over the sheet of paper, but there was no additional information on the back, no destination, no return date, no explanation of who was sick. Nothing.

He didn't know whether to be mad or worried.

He retrieved his cell phone and dialed her number.

It rang through to voice mail.

"Jenny," he said to the machine, struggling to keep his tone neutral. "It's me. I'm confused. Call me as soon as you can, okay?"

He hung up, waiting a long moment, took a deep breath, then pressed the speed dial for Cole.

Cole answered right away. "Maddison here."

"It's Mitch."

"Oh, hey, Mitch." There was definitely something off in Cole's tone. He knew something.

"I'm looking for Jenny," said Mitch, giving his friend one chance to be straight with him.

"Really?" Cole asked. "She's not at work?"

Mitch ran out of patience. "What the hell is going on?" he barked.

There was a long pause that only served to reinforce Mitch's suspicions.

"What do you mean?" asked Cole, his tone still carefully neutral.

Mitch's voice went to steel. "Where's Jenny?"

"I don't know."

"Bull. Emily has to know."

"She might," Cole replied. "But she didn't tell me."

Okay, this just got weirder by the second. "Where's Emily?"

"She's at work."

"So she's not the one who's sick? And she didn't go to some friend's place with Jenny?"

"No." Cole didn't elaborate.

"What did I miss?" Mitch demanded

"As far as I know, nothing."

"As far as you *know?* What kind of an answer is that?"

Cole's tone went back to normal. "They didn't tell me so I wouldn't have to lie to you. Something's obviously up, but I haven't a clue what it might be. Did you and Jenny fight? Did you do anything?"

"Like what?"

"I don't know, see a girl in D.C.? Maybe somebody saw you and—"

"I did *not* see a girl in D.C." Unless you counted the mental images of Jenny that followed him 24-7.

"Well, she took off for some reason," said Cole.

Mitch paced across the office. "Find out what it is. Talk to Emily."

Cole barked out a cold laugh. "You want me to compromise my relationship with my fiancée to help you?"

"Absolutely."

"You really don't know how these things work, do you?"

Mitch paused for a long second. "I'm learning," he admitted.

Cole went silent. "Elaborate."

Spill his guts? Own up to his feelings to Cole before he even told Jenny? "I don't think so."

"You want my help?"

Mitch punched the heel of his hand against the office wall. "Fine. There's a lecture from Jeffrey on squandering chances echoing inside my head, an engagement ring sitting in my jacket pocket and I'm ready to tear this state apart looking for Jenny."

"You bought an engagement ring?"

"Yes," Mitch hissed.

"You want to marry Jenny?"

"Who *else?*"

"Well, I don't know what the hell you did in D.C."

"I accepted a job and bought a ring."

Cole's tone turned to surprise. "You took the job?"

"Where is she, Cole? Help me find her."

The line was silent for long seconds. "Can I tell Emily you're proposing?"

"*No!* It's bad enough that you know before Jenny. You're not telling her best friend."

"I don't know how else I'm going to—"

"Lie, cheat, steal. I don't care."

"You're not asking much, are you?"

"I'd do it for you."

Cole hesitated a beat. "Fine. I'll talk to her tonight."

"Now."

"Tonight. Summon up a little patience. It's not my fault it took you this long to make up your mind."

"I didn't—" Fine. Mitch would own that mistake. He should have realized he was in love days and days ago. If he had, if he hadn't been such a stubborn idiot, he'd already be engaged to Jenny.

Assuming she'd have said yes.

Of course she'd have said yes.

He was sure of it.

Almost.

Jenny knew deep down inside that coming to Lake Angel had been the right decision. She was still nauseous in the morning, and it took her a good hour to get her stomach calmed down. People were bound to have noticed, especially Mitch.

He would have arrived back from D.C. yesterday. She'd kept her cell phone deliberately turned off. In her more optimistic moments, she was afraid he might try to call. But then pessimism would take over, and she was afraid he wouldn't bother.

She told herself it was better not to know. And, if he did

call, she'd probably break down and cry, confess everything, humiliate herself and back him into a corner where, heaven save them both, he might decide to try and do something noble.

She couldn't live with that.

So the cell phone was staying off.

It was nearly ten in the morning. She'd managed a slice of toast and some orange juice earlier, taking great care to eat slowly. Coffee was definitely out of the question. Just the thought of it made her stomach roil.

Now, she wandered through the compact two-bedroom lakefront cottage, opening up each of the windows and letting the breeze flow through. Emily's family truly did have the most beautiful, picturesque spot on the lake. The cottage was nestled into a small cove, backed by a lush green forest. A dock stretched out from the crescent strip of sandy beach that ended in big piles of jagged boulders on either side.

Other cottages were visible in the distance across the crystal-clear blue lake. When the sun went down, their lights twinkled on the airwaves. The neighbors on either side of the property seemed friendly, but not at all cloying. Mrs. Burroughs kept busy in her massive gardens, while the Claytons said they commuted most days to jobs in the nearby town of Rex Falls.

Jenny eased into the big cushioned wicker chair in the corner of the airy living room. She'd managed to keep down a prenatal vitamin this morning, and now she planned to sip her way through a glass of milk, taking up where she left off reading in a mystery novel. She forced herself to read her way through the words on the page, banishing her speculation on where Mitch was and what he was doing right now, and fighting the memories of their amazing days and nights together.

She could do this.

She focused.

Thirteen

Über-detective Norma Wessil had just broken into a luxury penthouse hotel suite, discovering the body of Terrance Milhouse, ex–hit man and prime suspect in the murder of socialite Bitsy Green. Terrance's body was in the bedroom, halfway out of the bed. The cops were on their way up the elevator. And Norma had foolishly touched the murder weapon, leaving her prints behind.

As Jenny read Norma's internal debate on whether to hide the weapon or wipe it clean, the door to the cottage suddenly burst wide open. Jenny nearly jumped out of her skin. Her head shot up, and her gaze focused on Mitch. *Mitch?* The book dropped to her lap.

She found her voice. "How on earth—"

"It was my fault," Cole confessed as he barreled in behind him.

Jenny jumped to her feet, backing toward the wall.

"What are you doing here?" Mitch demanded without preamble. "Why did you leave Royal?"

"What?" she rasped at Cole, her heart pounding fast, stomach contracting in dread.

"Don't blame Emily," Cole quickly elaborated. "I tricked her into giving you up."

"What?"

Emily had told Cole? Cole had told Mitch? Emily had actually betrayed her confidence?

Mitch was moving toward her. His blue-eyed gaze was compassionate and gentle. "Jenny," he breathed in what sounded like sympathy. She quickly realized he wasn't mad. He was something else entirely. And there was only one explanation. He knew she was pregnant.

No, no, no. This couldn't be happening. What had Emily done?

"Please don't blame Emily," Cole repeated.

Then Emily rushed in, breathing hard. "Jenny, please, I didn't mean to—"

But Jenny's brain was a haze of shock and fear. "Tell him *I was pregnant?*" she finished Emily's sentence.

The entire room went stock-still.

Emily cringed, and Mitch gave a long, slow blink.

"I tried to phone you," Emily put in helplessly.

"You're *pregnant?*" Mitch rasped.

Jenny opened her mouth, but nothing came out.

He hadn't known? Then what was he doing here?

Emily's hand went to her forehead. "I only told him where you were. I didn't…I wouldn't…"

Mitch stepped forward, blocking Jenny's view of Emily. His blue eyes had gone hard, and his mouth was grim. "You're pregnant? And you're hiding from me?"

Her world contracted to him alone. "I didn't—"

"Didn't what? Didn't want to tell me? Didn't think I deserved to know? What the hell is the matter with you?"

Jenny tried to swallow, battling a paper-dry throat. "You had made it abundantly clear," she managed, voice trembling, "that you weren't in this for the long-term. You didn't make a commitment, and I didn't ask you to make—"

"So you decided I was an irresponsible son of a bitch who'd walk out on a woman who was pregnant with my child?" He raked a hand through his hair. "What have I ever done, Jenny? What have I done to make you think so little of me?"

He didn't understand, and she wasn't explaining it right. "Don't you see?" she pleaded, fighting tears. "That's the point. I knew you wouldn't walk out on me. I knew you'd stay. I knew you'd try to be noble, and you'd hate me for it in the end." Her hand went to her stomach. "I can't live my parents' nightmare all over again."

His expression cleared, and his eyes softened, and his shoulders dropped from their tense position. "I'd never hate you, Jenny. I—"

"You can't change your feelings just because I'm having your baby." She gave a watery laugh. If only things worked that way. If only Mitch could feel about her the way she felt about him.

He reached for her hands. "But I don't have to—"

"You'd feel frustrated and trapped." She tried to tug away, but he wouldn't let her. "And you'd get angrier and angrier—"

"I would—"

"—until one day, the fighting would start. And it doesn't end, Mitch. The plates hit the wall one after the other, after the other." She involuntarily cringed at the last memory of her father's harsh voice, and her mother's helpless pleas. "In my house, my father finally started throwing the china cups. And then he walked out the door, and my mother told me it would be all right. We just have to clean it up."

Jenny stopped talking, breathing hard.

Mitch drew her toward him, his voice going soft and gentle. "I'm not your father, Jenny. He didn't love your mother. I love you. That's the difference."

She looked him fully in the eyes, knowing she had to be strong. If ever there was a moment in her life she had to say everything exactly right, this was it. "Words are easy, Mitch. Especially for you."

"You think I'm lying about loving you?"

"I think you want to be a good guy."

"I'm not a good guy."

"You are."

"And you are unbelievably stubborn." He smiled.

"You took a job in D.C.," Jenny accused. "How is that love? How is leaving me love?" Even as she spoke, she steeled herself against the persuasive words he was sure to speak.

"It is," he insisted.

"You don't even know what you're talking about."

"But I do."

Something tightened in Jenny's chest, but she warned herself not to believe him. Mitch was the consummate diplomat, and right now he thought his mission was to sway her. She had to stay strong for both of them.

Then his voice went lower, more intimate. "Love is when you know deep down in your soul that you're never going to look at another woman. It doesn't matter where you go, or what you do, or who propositions you. Your mind is full of one gorgeous, feisty, funny woman back in Royal, Texas, and she's spoiled you for the rest of the world."

He stopped and waited.

"You're *so* good at that," Jenny responded with all the emotional strength she could muster, fighting hard against the desire to buy into his fantasy. "What happens when it's time for you to talk your way out of my life?"

"Feel inside my pocket."

Her brows went up at the bizarre request. "Excuse me?"

He chuckled. "Not that pocket." Then he let go of one of her hands and tapped the breast pocket of his suit jacket. "Feel it."

Her mind still full of suspicion, she reached up. Gingerly, she pressed against the spot he'd indicated. It was a hard lump, and she shrugged her shoulders in incomprehension.

His mouth was curved into a smile as he reached inside and extracted a small box. It was pale green leather, almost silver in its sheen. He tilted it toward her, and she read the embossed words, "Marry Me."

Something the consistency of concrete slid through to the bottom of her stomach. It wasn't possible. There was no way.

Mitch lifted the lid to reveal a stunning diamond solitaire against a tiny satin pillow.

She blinked, while goose bumps tingled to life across her skin. "I don't understand?" she managed.

"Guys who aren't in love and who, by the way, have no earthly clue their girlfriends are pregnant, do not buy engagement rings and wander around with them in their pockets waiting for exactly the right moment."

"He's right about that," Cole put in, and Jenny saw Emily press an elbow into his ribs.

Mitch gave Jenny's hand a squeeze. "Will you marry me, Jenny? Please."

She gazed up at him. How could this be happening? He hadn't known she was pregnant. He'd had no idea there was any reason for him to be noble.

"I don't understand," she repeated.

His smile was tender, and his eyes shone blue-silver. "I love you, and I want you to marry me. And it has absolutely nothing to do with you being pregnant. Though, I'm thrilled about that. And I am going to be a fantastic father. And I am never, ever, *ever* leaving you, Jenny."

Tears formed in her eyes, and she glanced at Emily.

Emily was grinning ear to ear. "I believe the word you're looking for is *yes*."

Jenny shifted her incredulous gaze to Mitch. These weren't just words. He wasn't being diplomatic. He wasn't trying to make her feel good. He honestly—

She drew a shaky breath. "Yes."

He kissed her fast and hard and deep, and then scooped her up into his arms, glancing around. "Which one is your room?"

Jenny laughed in surprise, nodding to a door beside the kitchen.

"Excuse us," Mitch said over his shoulder to Cole and Emily.

"You might want to put the ring on her finger," Cole called from behind, laughter threading through his voice.

"Later," Mitch growled in Jenny's ear. "With flowers and champagne and me on one knee."

Lying in her cottage bed, Jenny gazed up at the diamond that sparkled on her finger. They hadn't bothered waiting for the flowers and champagne, hadn't even made it out of bed all afternoon. Emily and Cole had headed back to Royal, obviously seeing no reason to stick around and say goodbye.

Mitch's body was warm against Jenny's, a light sheet covering them both while the breeze from the ceiling fan wafted its way down.

His hand trailed over her stomach, cupping it with his warm palm. "So, I'm going to be a daddy."

She put her hand on top of his. "Yes, you are."

He kissed her temple. "You okay with all this?"

"I am now." She tipped her head to look at him. "You?"

"I'm not going to be like my father."

"And I'm not going to be like my mother."

His free arm went around her, and he gave her a squeeze. "We're going to do this right."

"And, apparently, we're going to do it in D.C.?"

"That was part of my plan. But only if you agree."

"It's a good job?" she asked, thinking she'd live anywhere in the world with Mitch. Sure, she had good friends in Royal, but Emily meant the most to her, and it looked like Emily's life was about to get very mobile. Cole had houses all over America, and in at least four other countries.

"It's a very good job," Mitch replied. "But you and the baby are my priority. We can stay in Royal if you want. I'll find something to do."

"Can we come back to visit?"

"As often as you want. We'll keep your house. Hell, we can keep mine if you'd rather. Two might be overkill."

"I do like my lot on the lakeshore," Jenny admitted. "And we'll have to teach the baby to swim somewhere."

"And there are those great French country house plans on your short list."

"I picked the other one."

"Not anymore you didn't."

Jenny couldn't help but smile at the conviction in his tone.

Mitch's hand flexed convulsively against her bare stomach. "A baby. It boggles the mind," he admitted in a whisper.

"Well, I'm excited."

"Yeah?" There was a salacious edge to his tone.

"Not that kind of excited."

He gave an exaggerated sigh. "Too bad."

"But I am hungry. I'm eating for two." She paused. "Well, one and a very little bit at the moment."

He drew her more comfortably into his arms. "It happened that very first night?"

"That very first night."

"It must have been fate."

"I think it was Emily's burgundy dress."

"That was Emily's dress?"

"Yes."

"You should buy it from her."

Jenny laughed. "You know, she's probably not going to want to wear it again."

"I'll make her an offer." Mitch glanced around. "I sure wish you had room service here."

"You better get up and cook me something. I'm in a delicate condition." For some reason, her stomach felt much stronger now.

He propped himself up on one elbow. "You need to eat?" Then he sat up and swung his legs over the edge of the bed. "What do you want? I'll make something right now."

She laughed. "Wow. This delicate condition thing is really going to work for me."

He turned and flicked his index finger across her nose. "No. This having Mitch Hayward in love with you is going to work for you."

"I'll take a cheeseburger, please."

He stood. "I'm bringing you a salad and a glass of milk with that."

His cell phone chimed from the pocket of his pants that had been discarded on the floor, and he bent to retrieve it.

He checked the display. "Cole."

"Tell them they didn't have to leave."

"Oh, yes, they did." He pressed a button. "Yeah?"

Mitch paused to listen for a moment, then he shifted the phone out of the way. "Cole wants to know if he can spill the beans. The temporary admin person heard that message on the office voice mail from D.C., and people are wondering where you've gone."

Jenny shrugged. She was over the moon with happiness. Cole could shout the news from the rooftops. In fact, if he didn't, she just might.

Mitch went back to the phone and said, "Go for it." Then he laughed. "Are you serious? Why?"

"What?" asked Jenny, but Mitch held up his index finger.

"It'll be up to Jenny," he said. He shook his head. "People are strange. Okay. Call you when we get back to town."

"What?" she asked after he'd signed off.

"Apparently, Brad is talking to Cole about making the Tigers' home city Royal and giving me a job in management."

"Wouldn't they have to build a stadium?"

"I suspect this had more to do with Brad distracting the

electorate from the blackmail issue than any serious bid for the team."

"Would you do it?" Jenny pulled back the covers and got out of bed herself. Burgers on the deck watching the sunset with Mitch would be fabulous.

"Up to you." Mitch stuffed one leg into his slacks.

"Do I have to decide now?"

"You absolutely do not have to decide now. I told the people in D.C. that I need a couple more months in Royal." He moved around the bed to where she was retrieving new underwear and pulled her into his arms. "I was hoping to spend it with you."

"Before you broke my heart?" She settled against his bare chest and the cool fabric of his slacks, reveling in the feel of his strong arms around her, wondering if dinner could wait.

"By that time, I'd come to the conclusion you'd be the one breaking mine."

"Never," she whispered, stretching up for a kiss that somehow went on and on.

Mitch was the one to pull back. "I *am* going to feed you," he vowed.

"It can wait."

"No, it can't. Our baby is hungry."

Jenny's heart melted into a pool of joy. "I love you, Mitch."

His expression sobered, and he gently cupped her cheek with his palm. "I love you so much, Jenny." Then he sighed. "Took me a long time to work that out, didn't it?"

The tenderness in his expression went straight through to her soul. "It doesn't matter. Not anymore. We have the rest of our lives together."

* * * * *

COMING NEXT MONTH

Available October 11, 2011

You can find more information on upcoming
Harlequin® titles, free excerpts and more at
www.HarlequinInsideRomance.com.

*Harlequin Romantic Suspense presents the latest book
in the scorching new* KELLEY LEGACY *miniseries
from best-loved veteran series author Carla Cassidy*

*Scandal is the name of the game as the Kelley family fights
to preserve their legacy, their hearts…and their lives.*

Read on for an excerpt from the fourth title
RANCHER UNDER COVER

*Available October 2011
from Harlequin Romantic Suspense*

"**W**ould you like a drink?" Caitlin asked as she walked
to the minibar in the corner of the room. She felt as if she
needed to chug a beer or two for courage.

"No, thanks. I'm not much of a drinking man," he
replied.

She raised an eyebrow and looked at him curiously as she
poured herself a glass of wine. "A ranch hand who doesn't
enjoy a drink? I think maybe that's a first."

He smiled easily. "There was a six-month period in my
life when I drank too much. I pulled myself out of the bottom of a bottle a little over seven years ago and I've never
looked back."

"That's admirable, to know you have a problem and then
fix it."

Those broad shoulders of his moved up and down in
an easy shrug. "I don't know how admirable it was, all I
knew at the time was that I had a choice to make between
living and dying and I decided living was definitely more
appealing."

She wanted to ask him what had happened preceding
that six-month period that had plunged him into the bottom

of the bottle, but she didn't want to know too much about him. Personal information might produce a false sense of intimacy that she didn't need, didn't want in her life.

"Please, sit down," she said, and gestured him to the table. She had never felt so on edge, so awkward in her life.

"After you," he replied.

She was aware of his gaze intensely focused on her as she rounded the table and sat in the chair, and she wanted to tell him to stop looking at her as if she were a delectable dessert he intended to savor later.

Watch Caitlin and Rhett's sensual saga unfold amidst the shocking, ripped-from-the-headlines drama of the Kelley Legacy miniseries in

RANCHER UNDER COVER

Available October 2011 only from Harlequin Romantic Suspense, wherever books are sold.

HRSEXP1011